With love, to
Jacquelyn Leigh Logan
whom we welcomed to the family
on August 3rd, 1989,
a sister for Nate and Jessica
and a cousin for Ashley, Courtney, and Katie.

Table of Contents

Trouble
In A Fur Coat

by Janette Oke

**Illustrated by
Brenda Mann**

Other Janette Oke
Children's Books in this Series

Spunky's Diary
New Kid In Town
The Prodigal Cat
Ducktails
The Impatient Turtle
A Cote of Many Colors
A Prairie Dog Town
Maury Had a Little Lamb
This Little Pig
Pordy's Prickly Problem
Who's New at the Zoo?

Trouble in Fur Coat
Copyright © 1990
Janette Oke
All Rights Reserved

Published by Bethany House Publishers
A Ministry of Bethany Fellowhship International
11400 Hampshire Avenue South
Minneapolis, Minnesota 55438
www.bethanyhouse.com

Cover Illustration by
Brenda Mann

Printed in the United States of America

ISBN 0-934998-38-8

Chapter One

Waking

I could sense the stirring beside me. I was used to my mother shifting from one side to another, or my tiny roommate nosing about in her sleep, but somehow, even in my sleepy state, I realized that something was different. There seemed to be more restlessness, more purpose in the moving about of my mother. I heard a deep, guttural grunt and she tossed her large, furry head to one side. I moved to nurse. That often had seemed to quiet and comfort her in the past, and she would stretch lazily and fall back into an easy sleep.

But she didn't respond in that way now. I heard her grunt again and she gently nosed me out of the way and lunged up onto all four feet.

My eyes opened wide with the shock of it. I had never seen my mother in any other position than spread out before me on the soft, dark ground of the den. I had not realized how mammoth she was. My eyes traveled upward in the semi-darkness that enfolded us and it seemed to me that they would never reach the top of her.

For just a moment it frightened me and then, sensing

my distress, she reached down and with her long pointed nose nuzzled me gently, whispering little endearments into my fluffy fur ear.

I felt better and pressed up against her. But I was still puzzled over why she abruptly stood, instead of rolling back onto her other side and resuming her nap.

My little sister had not stirred. I could hear her gentle breathing and I knew instinctively that I should not waken her. Mother had scolded us in the past when the one cried and disturbed the other.

I pressed close to Mother again, careful not to bump against the little furry ball that was my little sister. I wanted Mother to lay back down so that I might cuddle up against her, feeling warm and protected. Besides, I was hungry.

But Mother did not lie down. Instead she reached out with her sensitive nose and prodded my sister gently. The fur ball began to uncurl. A soft, fuzzy head lifted up, eyes wide with surprise and curiosity. Gradually a foot untangled, then another and another. Still the eyes stared unblinkingly at my mother. For a moment I could see the same fright that I had felt. The wide eyes seemed unable to believe what they were seeing. I wanted to giggle, having just been through the same experience, but I dared not.

My mother prodded her once more and I could hear the soft grunting of endearments. My sister responded then. She bounded up with great energy and threw herself at the large, dark form before her.

"Mother!" she cried in excitement.

I was as surprised as Mother by the sudden exhilaration. But Mother handled it well.

"Sh-h-h," she cautioned. "Sh-h-h. We never know who might be about."

It was the first that we had really conversed with one

another. Up until then Mother had let us know what she wanted simply by a push or a nuzzle. And I had never spoken to the other little furry ball that shared the bed with us in the den. Seeing her now, I felt excitement. She looked like she was going to be a lot of fun.

I pushed forward timidly, but eagerly, and reached out my nose toward her. She did giggle. Right out loud and Mother had to "sh-h-h" her again.

We both backed up a step and stood looking at one another. Up until then I had viewed her simply as someone that I had to share my dinner with—now I saw her as a possible playmate. The prospect excited me. For the moment I even forgot that I was hungry.

But Mother was moving again. Not to lie back down in a comfortable position on the den floor, but moving slowly along the confinement toward the spot where just a hint of light spilled into the small enclosure.

"Sh-h-h," she grunted to both of us, and we would not have moved—or even breathed, had the whole roof fallen in.

From where I stood I could sense the tension in every fiber of her being. Her eyes flashed, her nose twitched, and the muscles under her loose coat of fur rippled with each step.

"This is different," I said to myself. "Mother has never stood and moved about before."

She stopped again and stood sniffing. Her sharp ears were perked forward to catch the faintest sound. I heard sounds, too. Stirrings and callings—strange sounds when all had been silence for so long.

Then my mother did the strangest thing. With one large, clawed paw she reached out and swatted at the wall before her. It moved. What had seemed impenetrable a few moments before was suddenly a small opening. Limbs and boughs and shrubbery had been shoved aside.

Mother stopped and sniffed and listened again. Then she went to work once more in careful destruction. Soon there was a large opening before us. For a moment my eyes could not stand the sudden brightness. I looked away, blinking. It was then that I noticed my sister. She had backed up into a corner until her back was up against the dirt bank, her whole tiny body trembling. Her eyes were huge in her skinny little face and she looked scared half out of her wits. That was when I giggled.

"Sh-h-h," came Mother's sharp reprimand and I bit my tongue and scurried out of her reach.

Mother waited for a few moments, sniffing and listening. I cowered in one corner and my little sister crouched in another. We weren't sure what was happening in our world. We had experienced nothing like it before.

Then Mother stepped forward—slowly—cautiously—her big head rolled slowly from side to side. Her nose lifted even higher. She shifted her weight slightly from one foot to the other and made her circle of head movement again and again. At length she stepped back so that she was in the den.

"It's time," she said softly.

We were still puzzled. I suppose we both wanted to ask questions but we were still too unsettled, too nervous about the sudden changes in our lives.

Mother turned to the opening again. She seemed tense—anxious now. She sniffed and I saw the ripple of excitement pass through her. Suddenly I was no longer afraid. Something wonderful—something like nothing we had ever known before was about to happen. I was ready. I bounded forward, eager to get on with it, but a large paw moved like a flash and Mother pinned me rather roughly to the den floor.

"One never barges from the den," she scolded, and then softened somewhat. "There can be dangers out there. I'll go first. If all is safe—I'll call you."

Then she looked over at my sister who was still pushed up tightly against the wall, her eyes big, her body shaking. Mother changed quickly from a lean and shaggy body of agitation to a warm and comforting mother. She drew us both tenderly to her and snuggled us up against her.

"Before we go you'd better have your dinner," she soothed. "Once we are outside you may be so excited discovering things, that you'll even forget to eat."

I remembered how hungry I was then and I guess sister felt the same way for we both accepted Mother's invitation without argument. But I was anxious to get the meal over with so that I could get on with Mother's plans. They sounded most exciting. As we nursed hungrily she told us a little about the world beyond our den.

"There is much more to the forest than this small, confined hole," she said, and I could sense her tremble of excitement again.

I wanted to ask why we had never seen it before but I was much too busy eating.

"The world was buried in a heavy coat of white cloud," went on Mother. "It does that periodically. When it does, we bears know that it is time to sleep. But the thick white goes away after a season and the green things come again. Then it is Time. Time to stir. Time to leave. Time to feast again."

I'd had enough dinner. I couldn't wait any longer. I pushed back and, with a pink tongue, licked the last trace of nourishing milk from my chops.

"Then let's go," I urged Mother, trembling with my excitement.

"When Kimwa is finished," Mother said softly, but I sensed that she was even more impatient than I was.

It was the first that I had heard my sister called by name. It surprised me a bit. I glanced over at the little one who still nursed contentedly. "Kimwa," I thought. "It suits her."

Then Kimwa lifted her furry head, her eyes looking too big for her face. She still looked a little nervous but I saw a spark of adventure there too.

"Are you done?" I asked hopefully.

She just nodded, but her eyes began to sparkle.

I could scarcely contain myself—but I knew better than to go bursting toward the door of the den again. We both stepped back and waited for Mother. She didn't need to be encouraged. With lumbering step she moved toward the door again. She stopped, sniffed, listened, shifted her weight, tested the air, and then she was moving slowly from the den mouth, still sniffing and listening.

A tremble went all through my body. I tried to hold myself in check. I wondered if Kimwa felt as excited as I did. I found myself pressing up close against her and she in turn pressed up against me. I felt the tremble pass through our bodies. I wasn't sure if it had started with her or with me.

Then Mother's large head turned slightly. She smiled as she looked at us.

"Come," she nodded, and we both bounded forth from our winter prison.

Chapter Two

The New World

I could not believe my eyes. There before us stretched the most magnificent, the most incredible sight one could imagine. For a moment I felt that I was having some fantastic dream and then I heard Kimwa let out her breath in a long, deep sigh as she said, "Oh-h-h-h," and I knew that what I was seeing must be real.

"Oh-h-h," Kimwa said again. "Lo-o-o-k!"

I was too busy looking to pay much attention to Kimwa, but I did wish to share the excitement with her so I crowded up against her and together we let our eyes slowly adjust to all that we were seeing.

Near at hand large things reached right up to the sky, some with bare, gnarled fingers stretching out this way and that, others dressed in green prickly fur. All about us was a jumble of tangled things—little ones, big ones, bushy ones, skinny ones. I tried to sort the one from the other—but I couldn't really tell where the one stopped and the next started.

Then there were big and little lumps and mounds—hard ones and softer ones, brown ones and grey ones.

And beyond the big straight-upward-pointed-things and the hard-and-soft-colored-lumps, the ground began to slope away, deeper and deeper until one couldn't see where it all ended. And all the way along the slope were more tall and short things and more lumps and mounds.

Letting my gaze travel off further and further, I saw an upward slope, and then another and another, and they too were covered with all sorts of things.

I could stand it no longer.

"Mother," I cried, tugging on one big shaggy paw, "what is it all?"

She smiled. "You'll learn all about it in due time," she began.

"Tell us. Tell us," squealed Kimwa and I realized that she was as excited as I was.

"Such impatience," said Mother but she was still smiling.

"What's that?" I yelled, pointing at the nearest tall thing with bare giant fingers.

"That is a tree."

"What's that?" I swung around to point to the green prickly one.

"That is a tree also."

I blinked. Looking from the one to the other, Kimwa expressed my puzzlement.

"But they're different," she murmured.

"Yes," agreed Mother, "they are. There are many kinds of trees in the forest. If you can be patient you'll learn all about them."

"Is that a tree, too?" I asked, pointing to a group of tangled sticks.

"That is a bush," said Mother and to my alarm, she began to move slowly from where we had been standing. There were still all kinds of things around about us

that I hadn't learned the names of.

Something moved above our heads. It came from one of the trees and moved directly toward us and then veered off to the side and stopped in another tree.

"What's that?" I whispered, wondering if we were about to be attacked.

"That's a bird. There are many birds in the forest."

"Do they—do they hurt us?"

Mother laughed gently, "Oh, my no," she said. "The birds are our friends."

I was glad to hear that. I was about to say so when there was the strangest noise. It was loud and chattery and came from the tree closest to us. Both Kimwa and I automatically pressed ourselves against Mother.

"What's that?" I whispered, trembling.

"That's just a squirrel," answered Mother.

"But he—he sounds cross," I went on.

"He likely is cross," replied Mother. "Squirrels are always scolding for one reason or another. Pay no attention to him. This is our forest, too. We have as much right to be here as he does."

I looked up into the tree—and there he was. Why, he was no bigger than a minute. Even Kimwa was much bigger than he was. I smiled, no longer afraid.

"This is our forest, too," I called to him. He flicked his big bushy tail, dashed up the tree to a safer perch and turned to scold me again. I just laughed.

But Mother was moving on and I stopped teasing the angry squirrel and turned to follow her.

Around us were all sorts of things that I didn't know about. I did wish that Mother would stop and tell us about them.

"What's that?" I cried after her, pointing at one of the big lumps.

Mother barely swung her head to view my pointing

nose.

"That's a rock," she said almost absent-mindedly, "now come along."

"But—but—," I began to complain, but Kimwa was obediently following Mother and I knew that unless I wanted to be disciplined I'd better do likewise.

"Where are we going?" I asked when I could catch my breath.

"To the stream," answered Mother.

"What's a stream?" puffed Kimwa, having as much difficulty as I was in trying to keep up.

"You'll see," said Mother and we had to be content with that.

It was not easy making our way through the dense bushes and the rocks and other things that I hadn't discovered a name for. Both Kimwa and I puffed and panted as we hurried to keep up. Mother seemed in an awful hurry to get somewhere and there was so much I was seeing as we rushed on that I wanted to know about. But I had neither the time nor the breath to ask her. Inwardly I kept saying, "What's that? And what's that?" but my questions went unanswered.

It seemed that we traveled on and on and I was about to collapse with fatigue when I noticed Mother's steps slowing. I sensed, more than saw, her head lift and I knew that she was sniffing and listening carefully again. For a moment she hesitated and Kimwa tumbled into me as I made an abrupt stop.

"What is it?" she whispered, but Mother quickly hushed her.

I guessed that Mother didn't like what she smelled for she turned from the direction she had been traveling and began to move again in what turned out to be a large circle. Her head was held high and her ears alert and every now and then she would stop and listen and

sniff again.

At last we arrived at the edge of a place where the trees were not as thick and Mother stopped and sniffed again. Then she did a very strange thing. Something that I had never seen her do before. She lifted herself right up on her two back feet, her front paws dangling before her, and stood erect, sniffing and listening as her large head rolled again from side to side.

If we had thought that she was big when we first saw her standing on all four, she was doubly big now. I could see Kimwa's eyes widen again as they traveled up, up, until they at last reached the top of Mother's head. I wanted to giggle again but something told me that the moment was too serious for that.

Mother grunted then—a contented kind of sound—and dropped back down on all four. We began to move forward again. I guess she was assured that it was safe to do so.

Soon I could hear a new sound. It was strange and low and gurgling. I wondered what kind of animal laughed like that, but I didn't have time to ask for soon we came out into the open and the strange creature stretched out before us.

"What's that?" I said in a whisper, not sure if I should be talking, but too filled with wonder to control myself.

"This is the stream," said Mother and without a moment's hesitation she went right on walking toward it—and then right onto it—but she didn't walk on top. She walked right into it. It didn't even hold her up.

Kimwa and I just stopped in our tracks and stared. Would the strange stream gobble up Mother?

But Mother had stopped now and she lowered her head and began to noisily gobble up the stream.

Oh, not all of it. There was lots there and as much as

Mother drank, it never seemed to make a bit of difference. She just kept drinking and drinking and it never lessened any, or went away.

At last she stopped and looked at us.

"Come," she urged. "Come try the water."

I hesitated but Kimwa moved forward.

"I thought you said it was "stream," I reminded mother.

"I did," she laughed. "The stream is made up of water. The water is what we drink. The stream comes from somewhere beyond—and goes to somewhere yonder. We have never found a beginning—or an end."

Kimwa had reached the stream. She jumped back quickly when her front paw splashed into the water.

"It's cold," she cried.

"Not too cold," Mother encouraged.

"But it—it wants to bury me," said Kimwa in alarm. Mother laughed.

"And what if it does?" she said. "All us bears love to play in water."

"Play in it?" Kimwa stopped short. "I thought you said we drink it?"

"Oh, yes. Water is wonderful. We drink it and play in it."

Kimwa took one more step but she wasn't too convinced.

"Now hurry—both of you," Mother prompted again. "We have much to do and not much time. Get your drink before we move on."

I decided against my better judgment, I'd better give the water a try. Kimwa was just lowering her black nose when I put my first paw in. But she didn't drink long and hard like Mother. She jumped, and then sputtered, then choked and began to cough. I knew that Kimwa didn't care much for the water.

"Now try slowly," Mother admonished. "Little swallows, until you know how to drink."

Kimwa was still shaking her head and giving little grunting coughs.

"Like this," said Mother and she lowered her head again to show us how it was done.

I tried—a bit hesitantly. At first I just pretended to suck in a bit of the water. Then I actually did draw in—just a sip. It was cold and it was tasteless. I couldn't understand why Mother was so impressed with the stuff.

I took one more little sip to please Mother and then I made my way back out of it. I felt that I'd had enough for one day and my paws were getting cold.

I lifted each one high as I headed back to solid ground. First one, then the other, trying to get them above the water level as I took each step.

Kimwa tried to drink again, but she didn't do so well that time either and she left the stream, still coughing and sputtering. She was in such a hurry to escape from the water that she began to run and lunge as she left. Water flew in every direction, splashing all over my coat.

"Watch it!" I yelled at her. "You're getting me all wet and cold."

"Now Natook," scolded Mother. "Don't be such a crank."

I wondered momentarily why Mother had suddenly changed my sister's name and then I realized that she was speaking to me. I was Natook. I had never heard my name before. It seemed strange. I wanted some time to think about it but the splashing affected Kimwa in a strange way. With a gleam in her big eyes, she headed even closer toward me and I'm sure that she purposely whipped up even more of the wet, frigid water. I was doused from head to toe.

"Kimwa," I yelled at her with a warning in my voice.

But Kimwa rushed on past and right between the two front legs of Mother before she whirled around to look at me, the mischief gleaming in her eyes.

I gave her a threatening look as I carefully high-stepped the last little distance to the shore and began to shake and shudder to try to dislodge some of the heavy water from my fur coat.

Before I could spend much time complaining or threatening, Mother began to move again, calling us to follow.

I soon forgot my anger with Kimwa as I looked about me at all of the exciting things of the forest. Mother was not moving as quickly now and I felt that I might dare to ask a few questions.

"What's that?" I called, pointing to one of the many lumps of white stuff that lay scattered about us.

"That's snow," answered Mother. "It will soon be gone again now."

"Where does it go?" I asked her.

Mother shrugged her shaggy shoulders carelessly but there was a puzzled look in her eyes.

"No one knows," she said. "We never see it get up and travel. But it gets smaller and smaller—and then it's gone."

"Maybe it crawls right into the ground," offered Kimwa.

"Maybe," said Mother, "but it doesn't leave any hole."

I decided to investigate the snow before it up and disappeared before my eyes.

I stopped running just long enough to reach out my slender nose and sniff at it. There was really no smell. It didn't move—it didn't fight. It just lay there and let me poke at it.

It was funny stuff. It didn't stay all in one piece as I shoved my nose against it. In fact, some of it went right up my nose. I started sneezing and Mother turned her head to see what I was up to.

"Come," she told me and I left the snow as I'd been told, and galloped after her, still sneezing.

"What is it like?" asked Kimwa when I got close enough for her to whisper to me.

"Not worth bothering with," I assured her. "It doesn't do anything but get up your nose. It can't even hold its body in one piece. And it's cold."

"Like the water?"

"Even colder, I think."

"I wouldn't like it much," said Kimwa and I shook my head in agreement. I didn't like it much, either.

We hurried on after Mother. She seemed to be in a hurry again and it took all that we could do to try to keep pace with her.

At last she stopped and went through her sniffing routine. And then she proceeded cautiously and we were out of the heavy tree growth again. For a moment I feared that she had brought us to another stream. I hadn't been too impressed with the last one. In fact, if I hadn't been running so hard to keep up with Mother I was sure that I would have still been shivering.

But it was not a stream.

Chapter Three

A Disappointment

"What is this?" I asked Mother as my eyes traveled here and there over the empty space before us.

"This is the meadow," she informed us.

"Why did we come here?" asked Kimwa, looking nervously about. She didn't seem too anxious to expose herself in such a fashion!

"There are lots of good things to eat here," answered Mother, and moved forward again.

I guess Kimwa and I found it difficult to understand why we should need something to eat. Mother had always supplied for us quite adequately. But as I looked at Mother I noticed that her sides were gaunt and her coat hung loosely and I suddenly realized that Mother, herself, might indeed be hungry.

Mother moved to something lying on the ground.

"Here is one place to find food," she explained to us.

"What is it?" asked Kimwa.

"A log," answered Mother.

It sure didn't look very good to me—but I was willing to take Mother's word as truth. I reached out and sniffed at the thing before us. It didn't smell good at all. I shook my head, then stuck out my tongue and took a lick. It didn't taste good, either. I looked up at Mother, feeling some doubt about her judgment for the first time.

"Not the log, silly," laughed Mother. "We eat what we find under the log."

I blinked. Then I looked back at the big log laying before us and blinked again.

"How do we get under it?" I asked with frustration.

Mother laughed again but she didn't answer my question.

"Stand back—both of you," she said and we both scurried back a distance from the thing on the ground.

Mother lowered herself to the ground beside the log and then reached forward with her strong front paws. She paused just a moment and looked at us. "Now when this moves," she said, "you come running. We won't have much time."

I wondered how Mother was going to get the thing to move. It had seemed quite dead to me. But even while the questions were bouncing around in my mind, I saw Mother reach forward, grasp the log in her powerful front paws and give a mighty heave. The log rolled to the side and Mother lunged up and began to hurriedly push her nose back and forth over the ground that the log had covered, her long tongue swishing out this way and that as she scooped and shovelled and then smacked and chomped. I stood watching in wonderment. It seemed that she was greatly enjoying whatever she had found.

But what she'd found I did not know. In my awe at the scene before me, I had quite forgotten to run.

Kimwa hadn't. She was right there with Mother, her little head twisting back and forth, this way, then that as she tried hard to keep up with all of the commotion.

But I never once saw Kimwa's tongue appear.

And then Mother was grunting and pushing around with her nose and I knew that the action was all over. She at last left the remains of whatever had been under the log and moved off deeper into the meadow.

I came to my senses then and moved forward to join the puzzled Kimwa.

"What was it?" I whispered, hoping I wouldn't draw Mother's attention to the fact that I had not obeyed.

"I don't know," replied Kimwa, still shaking her head. "Things were just scurrying this way and that way—all at the same time."

"What things?" I persisted.

"I don't know. I'd never seen them before."

"Well—what did they look like?" I felt a bit impatient with Kimwa. She had been standing there watching all of the action. Surely she had learned something.

"Little. Really little. And they moved so fast. You could hardly see them. Just a—a flick here and a flash there—and they were gone."

"They were gone 'cause Mother ate them," I informed Kimwa, with a sneer.

"Not all of them," Kimwa said defiantly. "Some of them got away."

"Got away where?"

"I don't know. They just disappeared—in little holes or something."

"Did they do like the snow?"

But Kimwa shrugged her shoulders and moved to follow Mother.

I shrugged too and followed along after both of them. I wished that I had been there to see the action. It sounded rather exciting. I decided that the next time Mother gave an order, I'd be a little more careful to obey it.

Mother must have covered miles in her effort to find food. Log after log was rolled over. The few things that went scurrying at the interruption of their nap, were hardly enough to taste, let alone satisfy a bear-sized appetite. Mother seemed to get more tense and more cross as the day wore on. Kimwa and I were wise enough to stop pestering her with our countless questions.

We couldn't resist doing a little nosing around on our own. But we didn't get very far in our little journeys. Each time that we got a few feet away from Mother we were sharply reprimanded and we came scurrying back. We couldn't really understand why she was so concerned. There was nothing to harm us in the forest. As Mother had said, it was ours. Surely we could do as we wished.

But in spite of my reasoning, Mother kept a sharp lookout. Every few minutes I would see her lift her head and sniff carefully in all directions. Her ears would flick forward as though straining for any sound. On a few occasions she even lifted herself upright, standing way above us on her hind feet. My, she looked big whenever she did that. Kimwa and I couldn't quite get used to it and we crowded together, staring up at the large form that was our mother.

Kimwa and I were not dependent on the few bugs and larvae that Mother uncovered when she rolled a log—though I did taste them just to see if I'd like them. They were good, just as Mother had said, but they were so hard to catch that I often gave up and let Mother do the feeding. When we got hungry, we just told Mother and, rather reluctantly it seemed, she stopped her wild search for food and rested long enough for us to nurse.

I always felt like a good long nap after eating, but Mother didn't allow that. She prodded us both up and onto our feet and we started off again. I was really getting tired and I guess Kimwa was too for she started to get whiny.

Mother wasn't too patient with the complaining. She told Kimwa to "hush" and kept right on searching for promising logs.

Mother rolled another log and feasted under it, smacking and chomping. It was a particularly good one because the ants had built a small hill right up against it. When Mother tossed the log aside, the ants were exposed. I had never seen Mother so excited nor so quick in her working. Back and forth went her huge head and her long tongue as she scooped mouthful after mouthful. Kimwa and I had both tired of the game of trying to catch things and as soon as Mother rolled the log, we snuggled up together, too tired to play and too cold to explore and watched the action. It didn't take long. Anything that Mother didn't catch in the first few minutes was gone from sight in a flash.

Mother was still licking her lips when she turned to look for us. I guess she could see how tired we were for she didn't urge us to hurry and follow. Instead she let her eyes travel upward. I looked up, too. The sky above us had become very dark. Little bits of white stuff were slowly drifting down toward us. It was almost dizzying in its effect.

Mother sniffed.

She turned to us then and seemed to study us carefully.

"We need to get back to the den." She spoke as though to herself.

My head lifted. I was tired, it was true. And I was cold, too. It seemed to me that it was much colder than it had been when we had left our home that morning. But I didn't know if I was ready to go back to bed. I mean, the den was small. It was dark. It was crowded. I liked the big, exciting, outdoor forest much better.

"Come," said Mother, and Kimwa and I knew that we must obey.

Mother didn't even stop to hunt on the way back to the den. But she had covered so much area when she had been hunting that I was sure that she'd never find our den again. We had been traveling all morning and we had gone in one direction and then another, round and round and over here, then there. I had no idea where the den might be. I was sure that Mother must have lost track of it as well.

But Mother moved as though sure of herself. She did seem concerned about the white stuff that was now falling thickly all around us. When we crossed a meadow—I wasn't at all sure if it was the one we had crossed earlier in the day for I couldn't see well to get my bearings—the white stuff lashed into our faces, blown by a stinging wind. I was glad to get in the shelter of the trees again.

I could hear Kimwa whimpering as she scrambled to keep up with Mother. I didn't blame her. I even felt like joining her in her complaints.

On we ran, trying our hardest to keep pace with Mother. The white stuff was getting deeper and deeper, and I began to fear that I might just fall into it and get buried and Mother would never find me again. And just when I was so tired that I feared that I might drop in my tracks, Mother stopped her hurried walk and began to fumble and dig at the bushes before us. Then she turned to us and said softly, "Go in. Get out of the cold and snow."

I just looked at her. And then I looked at the white stuff all around us. So it was snow. I thought that snow lay in piles upon the ground, waiting for a chance to just sneak away in some unknown fashion when no one was looking. This stuff was coming right out of the sky. I couldn't understand snow. It was sneaky stuff. It came from who-knows-where and it went to who-knows-where. I decided that I'd like to discover the mystery. I'd catch snow when it least expected and find out where it went and when. I'd find out where it came from, too, if—. But Mother was pushing at me with her nose.

"Go in," she insisted and she sounded a bit impatient.

I moved. Kimwa was already in the den, shivering with cold and whining that she was hungry again.

Mother followed right behind us. She stopped long enough to pull some of the tangled branches up against our door and patted things into place with her long nose. Then she turned to us. She sat down on our familiar bed and drew both of us to her. Her long tongue began to remove the snow from our coats as we snuggled up against the warmth of her body and began to hungrily take our dinner.

My, I was hungry—and tired—and cold. I hadn't realized just how much, until I lay there against Mother and fed and rested and began to thaw out.

As the minutes ticked by and my tummy filled and my body warmed, I began to think again of the excitement of the day we had just experienced. We had discovered so many things and I knew instinctively that there was much more to be discovered. I could hardly wait to get out there again.

But I was so sleepy. My eyes wouldn't stay open and I could feel my body relaxing up against Mother. Kimwa was already asleep. I could hear her gentle breathing and feel her body rise and fall against me.

"Mother," I murmured in my contented state, "it's nice in the forest."

Mother grunted.

"I like it out there with the trees and the bushes and lose the birds and—." I was beginning to lose my concentration. "I can hardly wait to go back out tomorrow," I managed.

Mother shifted her weight slightly. She sounded as tired as I was. "We won't be going back out tomorrow, I'm afraid," she managed to answer me.

I struggled to draw back to see if she was serious but I was wedged in between one of her large paws and Kimwa.

"Why?" I asked from my imprisoned position. "I liked it out there in the—."

"Sh-h-h," said Mother. "You'll awaken your sister."

It was then that I realized that I had raised my voice.

"But why?" I repeated in a coarse whisper. "I—."

"I know," said Mother in a sleepy voice. "I like it out there, too. And we'll go again—just as soon as we can. But not tomorrow. The snow has come again. We must wait for it to leave."

"But—," I began.

"Sh-h-h," said Mother. "We need to sleep now."

I tried to settle down but I was still upset about the snow. What made it think that it could come and go whenever it wished and order us back to bed in the den? I was angry about the snow. If I ever discovered where it came from I'd just turn it right "off" and then I'd come and go as I wished.

I guess Mother could still feel the tension in my body.

"Try to rest," she said to me. "There's no use fretting about the snow. Eventually it will leave for good. It always does. We'll go out again then. Just be patient."

That was easy for Mother to say. She had been to the forest many times. She knew by name all of the

things that I was just discovering. Maybe they were so familiar that she even found them boring. But I was just learning about them. I was anxious to discover what they were and what they did and how they fit into our lives. I didn't want to spend more days curled up in the crowded, dimly lit den. I wanted to be out in the fresh air and the sunshine, with birds flitting about from tree to tree and squirrels scolding at me from nearby branches.

I still held myself rigid thinking of the way the snow was spoiling all of my fun.

Mother moved again and gently pulled me up closer against her. Kimwa breathed a contented little sigh and snuggled up against my back.

It was so nice and warm and cozy in the den. I was glad that Mother had found it again. I was glad that we could all curl up together and—. But I was getting sleepier and sleepier. I didn't even feel angry any more. I just felt so-o tired.

Chapter Four

Trying Again

The next several days were strange. I don't recall much about them—except that we woke on occasion and stirred about some. I don't remember us having any long talks or anything like that. But we would grunt and sometimes scold one another for crowding, or turn ourselves over to a more comfortable position. Kimwa and I spent time nursing and Mother would smack her lips and flick out her tongue as though she was terribly impatient to get back to turning logs.

Then we would settle back down and sleep some more. No one really seemed to be awake—yet we weren't deeply asleep, either. It was almost an in-between state, and one not totally enjoyable.

At last Mother rolled over and pushed herself up into a sitting position. Her movement wakened both Kimwa and me. I guess we were surprised all over again at the size of her, for we both stared at her with big, wide-open eyes.

She sat there, yawning and smacking, and then she seemed to become more wide awake. She reached over and nuzzled us, making sure that we were both alright.

Then she slowly lifted herself and moved toward the door of the den.

It took her a few minutes to remove the covering, but when she had it lifted from its place she seemed quite happy with what she found. Her satisfied grunt brought both Kimwa and myself to our feet. We wanted to see it for ourselves.

The world had changed again. The piles of white snow that had nearly buried us on our previous trip out had disappeared. Oh, there were still small piles of it here and there, but it was no longer a blanket, covering everything.

Beyond the den birds flitted, as though in a spirit of excitement. I could hear them twittering and calling and I could sense the eagerness in their voices. Suddenly I could hardly stand it. I pushed up against Mother, hoping that I could urge her out of the den once more.

But she didn't seem to notice my prompting. She yawned and smacked her lips once more.

"Can we go now?" I asked impatiently.

Her eyes turned to me. I thought for a moment that I was about to be scolded, but she smiled understandingly and nuzzled me gently back from the door.

"Remember the rules," she reminded me. "We do not leave the den until we are sure that it is safe to do so."

She moved forward, just far enough to push her long nose out the opening, and she began her sniffing and listening.

I remembered then and I moved to a position between her front legs and lifted my own nose. I could smell so many things—but they all smelled good—and tremendously exciting—to me.

Kimwa joined us. She sniffed in noisy little gasps.

First this way and then that. It sounded so funny to hear her puffing and panting beside me and soon I could resist no longer.

"Not like that," I giggled, giving Kimwa a playful push that sent us both sprawling at Mother's feet and we lay there and rolled and giggled together.

Mother stepped over us and out into the forest world. That stopped our playing. We sure didn't want to miss any of the excitement of the new day. We scampered to our feet and were about to burst out into the light when Mother's voice stopped us.

"Stop!"

We stopped. Right in the middle of our tracks.

Mother was backing slowly into the den again. Her nose was still sniffing, her ears pressed forward in an effort to hear every sound. She continued to stand— motionless, straining.

"What is it?" I finally managed in a whisper.

"I don't know," she answered me, "but the birds have become quiet and there is a strange smell. One I have not known."

"It's probably that stupid snow," I wanted to explode, but I didn't dare say a word. I could sense that Mother was very tense.

"Lie back down," said Mother at last and she moved to replace some of the covering at our door.

I could have cried—I was so disappointed. So angry. But I followed Kimwa back to our bed and lay down. Mother soon joined us. I guess she knew how we felt for she pulled us close and comforted us. We decided to eat again. I was still angry, but gradually I began to relax. I guess I slept for awhile. Mother's stirring awakened me. Outside the den I could hear the birds again. I wanted to bound up and see what was going on but I knew better.

Mother stirred about in the den for a few minutes before she moved toward the door. Then she cautiously lifted the screening and poked her nose out just a fraction. Then her whole head moved out the opening.

"Stay where you are," she said to Kimwa and me, and she moved forward slowly, one lumbering step after another.

She must have checked long and carefully. At least it seemed to me that many minutes went by before we finally heard her call us softly. We moved then to the door, eager to be out in the world, but careful to follow Mother's orders.

"You may come," she called to us. "Everything seems fine now."

We bounded forth, tripping over one another in our hurry.

The birds were there. They passed from tree to tree, noisy in their visiting. The squirrel scampered to the very tip of a limb overhead and said some nasty things to Mother—which she totally ignored. The rocks and logs looked just as we had left them, but for some strange reason, the forest smelled different to me.

Maybe Mother noticed it, too, for I saw her lift her head and sniff long and hard. Then she rolled it in another direction and did it again. She didn't seem concerned about the smell. In fact, she seemed pleased. She turned to us, excitement in her voice and said, "Come."

"Where are we going?" I asked, glad to scamper after her.

"To the stream," she replied and moved off quickly through the dense forest.

I remembered the stream. It was cold. But Mother liked it, so I was glad to follow.

Kimwa seemed just as excited as I was as we bounded through the forest trying to keep pace with Mother.

"Remember what those are?" Kimwa asked me, pointing to two birds that went sailing overhead.

"Birds," I answered.

"Right," said Kimwa as though she was an authority on them.

I felt just a bit annoyed.

"Remember what that is?" she asked, pointing to some bushes.

"Bushes," I replied.

"Right," she said again with such smugness that I couldn't let it pass.

"Stop acting so smart," I hissed and gave her a sharp push that sent her head-over-heels.

"Mother," screamed Kimwa and began to whimper so that Mother would look. I knew that she wasn't hurt. She hadn't fallen that hard.

Mother stopped and looked back, but she didn't say anything, just gave me a frown that said I'd better be good and I hung my head so that I wouldn't need to meet her eyes, and took my place at her heels.

Kimwa quickly forgot her little fall. She even seemed to forget that I had caused it. She was soon there at my side, pestering me again.

"Remember what was under the logs?" she asked me.

I gave her a dark look but she didn't seem to notice.

"Bugs!" she exclaimed, not even waiting for my answer. "Bugs and ants and things." She seemed pleased with her recollection. "Mother loves them," she went on, and then I realized that Kimwa was merely playing a little game of "remember," and rather than getting cross I decided to join in.

"Remember the snow banks?" I asked her.

"There still are a few," she noticed, looking around us.

I was glad that there was still some snow left. I wanted to sneak up on it and discover just how it disappeared. But I was glad that it wasn't all over the ground though. I was still angry with it for keeping us locked up in our den for so long.

"Remember—," began Kimwa but just then Mother silenced us and drew us to a halt.

"What is it?" I whispered when I dared to speak.

Mother was busy testing the wind again, but she did stop long enough to answer my question.

"We are nearly at the stream" she said. "Don't you hear it?"

I did hear something. It was a strange sound—like a low roaring and rumbling, with tumbling and gurgling all mixed in.

"Is that the stream?" I asked Mother, my eyes wide and my ears straining.

"That's the stream," she assured me.

"But—but it didn't do that before," I reminded her.

"That's because the last time we visited it, much of it was under the ice and snow," Mother explained. "The stream will be much different now." And she smiled as though she could hardly wait to show us the stream.

When she was totally satisfied that it was safe to do so, she moved forward again and we followed after her.

As we rounded some bushes I couldn't believe my eyes. There before us was a wide, tumbling expanse of hurrying water. It rumbled and gurgled and whipped itself into a real frenzy. Both Kimwa and I just stood and stared.

"We're—we're not going into it, are we?" stammered Kimwa, and I shared her fears. Surely this boiling water would dash us against the rocks that protruded in spots

through the splashing foam, and then carry us away with it.

"No," Mother assured us. "No, we won't go in it here. We'll go downstream where it flows much quieter. It's quite safe there."

I breathed a sigh of relief and moved away from Kimwa's trembling side.

Mother led us through the bushes alongside the stream. We traveled beside the tumbling water until we came to a spot where the stream widened and became quiet and tranquil.

"Here," said Mother. "We will stop here." And she waded right out into the water and began to drink deeply of the cold stream.

Kimwa and I both hesitated for a moment and then we too walked out into the stream and dipped in our noses.

It wasn't quite as cold as it had been earlier in the spring, but it was still plenty cold. I was finished much sooner than Mother. I began to make my way back to shore when I remembered how Kimwa had splashed me the last time we had been at the stream. I owed her one.

I looked around to see if Mother was watching. She was still busy drinking. I looked at Kimwa then. She stood close by, still delicately sipping.

"Remember—," I said softly, my eyes lighting up with my secret plan, "remember when we visited the stream before—and you splashed me?" and with the rush of the last few words I took my paw and swished it through the water, making the spray fly with a mighty splash all over the startled Kimwa.

But she didn't respond with a cry like I had expected her to. Instead, she answered with a squeal of delight and quickly swiped out with her own little paw and caught me with a stream of water, full in my face. The war was on then and we splashed and pushed and tumbled about in the water until we were both soaking wet.

Mother never even tried to stop us. She just went on drinking. I had the feeling that she lifted her head and looked at us now and then, but I was much too busy trying to get the best of Kimwa to know for sure. She was a real scrapper for such a tiny little thing. It was all that I could do to brace myself against her attacks. We tumbled and splashed and threw water at one another until we were so tired we could hardly lift a paw—still we did not stop.

It was Mother who halted the game.

"Come," she said. "We must eat."

Kimwa and I moved from the water, shaking as much of it from our furry coats as we could, then we followed Mother into the bush. We knew that we would be spending a day rolling logs again. But we hadn't gone very many steps when Mother stopped and poked her nose into some green stuff by the trail. She seemed happy with her find and pulled some of the greenery with her teeth and began to eat it.

I moved up beside her, watching her take another mouthful.

"What's that?" I asked her.

"Spring is here," she said with a smile and a nod of her big head.

"Where?" I asked quickly, looking all around us. I didn't see anyone.

Mother smiled. "You can't see Spring," she said.

"Then how do you know he's here?" I asked with puzzlement.

"You know because the world changes when Spring comes. There will be more things to eat now. See?

Things are beginning to grow. This is a plant."

"Are plants good to eat?" asked Kimwa.

"Not all of them," responded Mother. "But I'll show you the ones that are. Take this one, here. It's good. This one is not. Never eat this one. But the one that I am eating is good. Try some. Go on. Try it," she urged when we hesitated.

Kimwa was the first to try it. She looked a bit uncertain at first, but when she reached down for another bite I decided to try it too. It did taste rather good. I had another bite, and then Mother was moving on again. It was time to do some serious eating. It had been a long, long winter and it would take many days for her to fill out the sides of her heavy, brown coat again.

Chapter Five

Kimwa

We spent many days traveling over the hillsides while Mother foraged for food. When she found something tasty she shared it with Kimwa and me. Some of the things were delicious—some I felt demanded an "acquired taste." But Mother seemed to enjoy it all. She fed on so many different foods that I wondered how she had learned about them all. Kimwa and I still preferred our meal of milk.

At night we returned to the warmth and snugness of the den. It no longer worried me for I knew that the next morning we would be released to the world of the forest again.

Daily the world about us seemed to change. Even the trees were getting greenery now. I asked Mother about it and she called them leaves.

"It happens every spring," she told us.

Kimwa looked puzzled. "How can it happen every spring?" she wanted to know. "There was nothing there."

"True," said Mother. "They come in the spring, they leave in the fall."

"Where do they go?" I asked, wondering if the leaves were like the snow. Hardly any snow was around anymore, and try as I might, I had not discovered where it had been sneaking off to hide.

"They fall," said Mother. "They fall to the forest floor. We used a number of them to make our winter bed."

I looked at the ground beneath me. I could see shapes of things beneath my feet but they did not look at all green like the leaves above my head. For one moment I was sure that Mother was a bit confused.

"They change their color first," went on Mother. "They turn yellow and red and brown—and then they just drift down to the forest floor and rest there. They make a nice, soft bed."

I looked at the strange things beneath my feet again and leaned down to push them about with my nose. They smelled musty—just like our bed. They made me sneeze.

"That's very strange," Kimwa was saying, and I had to agree with her.

But the new leaves were not the only changes in the forest. There were new birds. The colors and songs were different from the first birds we had met. And they all seemed in such a twitter. They were flitting here and there, always in a hurry. Mother said that they were "nesting" and it seemed to be a happy experience for them, for wherever they were, they sang.

Even the squirrel seemed less saucy. I noticed another squirrel had joined her in the tree. They didn't seem to have much time to just stand around and scold, for both seemed busy scurrying here and there with some purpose in mind, unbeknown to us.

Kimwa and I were changing, too, though at the time we weren't aware of it. I could see that she was growing although she still wasn't very big compared to Mother. I guess I was growing, too.

I was discovering more each day about Kimwa. She was so much fun to play with. I was glad that Mother had arranged for her to share my days. Even though she was a girl, she was daring. And she was scrappy. She never complained much if I got a bit too rough. She just gave me a sharp nip with her little teeth as a quick reminder that I should be more careful. I was, too. Kimwa's little nips could take a piece out of one.

But generally we got along just fine. And Mother was usually content to let us wrestle and roll and tumble our way through the spring days.

There were times though when she would sharply remind us that we were getting a bit too careless in our play and would come to harm if we didn't pay a bit more attention, and we'd settle down for a time again until we'd forget her scolding and become reckless again.

The trouble was really Kimwa. She was the one who liked to push things to the limit. She was always daring me to do things—and of course, being a boy, I couldn't let Kimwa out-do me in anything.

"Bet I can beat you to that rock," she'd say, and before I could gather myself together or even decide which rock she had in mind, she'd be off and I'd be forced to try to catch up to her before she made it to her chosen rock.

Then she'd hoist herself up on the rock and chant at me, "I beat. I beat."

I'd end up trying to push her off the rock so that I could claim the spot, and a shoving match would result. Sometimes we settled it ourselves but at other times, Mother had to intervene.

In a few minutes Kimwa would be at it again.

"Bet I can roll a log over before you can."

Of course she had already picked her little log, made good and sure it would roll easily and had her paw underneath, before my eyes even had time to scan the vicinity for a promising log.

"I beat. I beat," she'd yell and I'd shove her aside so that I could steal the bugs while she was doing her boasting.

As soon as she realized what was happening she'd come flying at me, pushing me away so that she could eat her own find. Of course we'd squabble and by the time we got back to the bugs, they had all disappeared.

"It's your fault," Kimwa would say, cuffing me, and then I'd cuff her back and soon we'd be rolling and tumbling on the ground. It usually ended up in a playful wrestling match, with Kimwa giggling and me laughing—but occasionally one of us would get cross and then the little war would be ended by Mother.

Our games and little fights were all quite harmless. We enjoyed the tumbling about on the forest floor— and Mother made short work of the disputes. No harm was ever done. That is, until we discovered that we could climb trees. Kimwa had to push that to the limit, too.

It all started one day when Mother had noticed a peculiar smell in the area. She had sniffed and grunted in her alarm. And then there was a crackling of undergrowth and Mother had turned to us and given a sharp order, "Quickly! Up a tree."

Kimwa and I didn't even stop to wonder if it was possible for us to get up a tree. We both turned to the tree nearest to us and scampered for our lives. Mother seemed to just disappear into the nearby bushes.

Some creatures passed by a few moments later, noisily making their way down a trail that led to the stream. Kimwa and I clung to our perches, nervously sniffing the air, frightened half to death.

But the creatures seemed unaware of our presence. Mother said later that their noses are very poor at detection.

They had been gone for some time when Mother reappeared. She wasted no time in ordering us down from the trees and then quickly moved us off through the forest.

"What was it?" I asked when we had traveled beyond the spot.

"Hikers," she answered and I could see that the bristles on her neck had still not settled.

"Where were they going?" asked Kimwa.

"To the stream."

"But it's our stream," stated Kimwa indignantly.

"We must share," said Mother, but she didn't sound too excited about sharing.

"What do they do at the stream?" went on Kimwa.

"Nothing," said Mother. "I've never seen them do anything. They just look. They don't drink. They don't bathe. They sometimes fish.

"What's fish?" I asked quickly.

"You will soon learn," Mother informed us. "I will show you."

But Kimwa had already turned her interest to other things. I could see her looking upward, studying the tops of the tallest trees.

As soon as Mother felt safe from the hikers, she stopped to feed again. Kimwa waited until Mother was busy with the contents from under another log, and then she pressed close to me.

"Bet you I can climb higher than you can," she whispered and I knew that she had already picked out her tree.

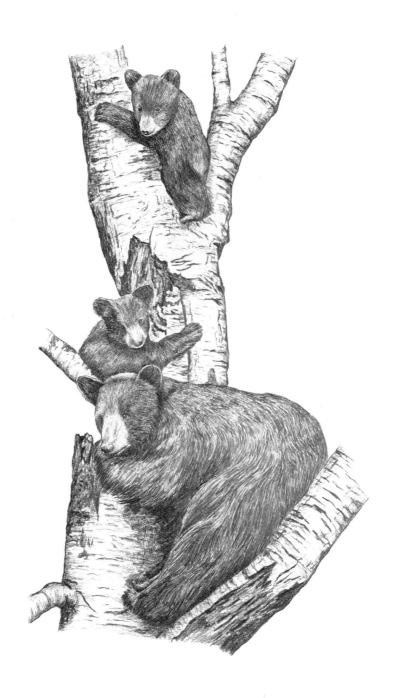

"Bet you can't," I countered, looking around me for what might be the highest top.

But Kimwa was already on her way. I could tell from the direction she was heading where to look for the highest tree. Right across from us was a dead pine that seemed to reach up to the very clouds. I wasn't going to be outsmarted by my little sister. I ran for the same tree.

She had a head start, but I was a bit faster. We reached the tree at about the same time and both began to climb.

I was the stronger so I began to get a slight lead, but then I remembered that Kimwa's dare was to climb the highest—not the quickest. I looked upward. The top of the tree narrowed to a small upward point. There would not be room for two bear cubs at the top, like there was on the base of the broad trunk. To beat Kimwa in her dare, I simply had to be up there first. That would crowd Kimwa out of the running.

I put on a burst of speed and managed to get ahead of her. I could hear her panting and scratching behind me. She was close. In one quick maneuver, I switched my position on the tree trunk so that I now was in front of Kimwa rather than at her side, blocking her way so that she couldn't pass me. Already the trunk had become much smaller and soon it would be too small for two bears to climb side by side.

Kimwa protested when I crowded in front of her.

"That's not fair," she yelled at me. "This is my tree."

"You said the highest," I answered in defense. "This tree is the highest."

"But you're not climbing fair," she panted, trying hard to push past me.

The tree was swaying slightly now. I could feel it trembling beneath me as I continued up, up. I looked down. Mother was way beneath us—still rolling logs and stones.

On I went, Kimwa close behind me. The tree swayed more and more. I slowed down now. I knew that Kimwa could never pass me on such a slender trunk. I guess she knew it, too, for I sensed that she had stopped climbing and was watching me make my ascent.

I wasn't going to be outdone by any girl. Kimwa might be sneaky—but I had outsmarted her. I was pleased with myself.

I continued to push my way up the slim point of the tree—higher and higher. I had never been so high before. It was almost dizzying. I looked down—way down—and saw Mother lift her head and look up.

I guess she sensed the danger long before I did, for I heard her nervous grunt and then she was moving quickly to the bottom of the tree.

"Come down," she called. "Come down at once."

I stopped climbing and tried to shift my weight slightly so that I could begin my descent. I felt a bit cheated. I had come so close to the top of the tree. Well, I had still beat Kimwa. I had climbed a good ten feet higher than she had. Reluctantly I began to back down.

And then there was a strange cracking sound. I swayed for just a moment, clinging wildly to the bit of tree trunk that I held in my paws. But I was moving. Strangely moving. I clung still harder. If I wasn't careful I would fall. And then I realized that I was falling—even though I still held tenaciously to the scrap of tree trunk. It had broken and it was falling, with me still hanging on.

"Let go," yelled Mother. "Let go and grab for a branch."

I tried to let go. I really did. I did manage to get one

paw free. I remember grabbing as I fell. I remember passing Kimwa on my way down. I remember her scream. I remember slamming into one branch after another, bouncing from this one to that one, hurting first this spot and then that spot. I remember the grunts being beaten out of me as I struck tree limb after tree limb, and I remember thinking that I was going to be killed for sure.

The next thing I knew I was at the stream. Mother held me. I was cold—and I was hurting all over. It felt like I had broken every bone in my body. Kimwa was there too. I could hear her whimpering softly.

"Is he gonna be alright?" I heard her ask Mother.

"I don't know," Mother answered truthfully, fearfully. "He had a nasty fall."

I felt the water swish over my head again and I gulped for some air.

"He's waking," said Mother, excitement in her voice.

"I'm cold," I protested, trying to free myself from Mother's grasp.

"Sh-h-h," she soothed me. "The cold water will help your bruises."

"But I'm freezing," I insisted.

"You'll warm up," said Mother, "later."

In spite of the fact that I shivered until my jaws shook, Mother kept me in the stream for some time. Then she lifted me carefully and carried me to shore. She placed me gently on the ground in a clump of low bushes and began to dry me off with her tongue, pulling me close against her warm body. Kimwa crowded in too, still whimpering that she was sorry.

Mother nursed us then and I fell asleep, still aching all over. I had never hurt in so many places. I was sure that I'd never be able to move again.

I was still sure of it when I awoke the next morning. My, how I hurt. I moaned and groaned with every move I made.

Mother fed nearby and came often to check on me. She coaxed me to the stream a couple of times and had me soak my sore bones and muscles.

"It will help," she promised me when I protested.

Maybe it did help, I don't know. But I do know that it was several days before I could properly walk again, and much longer before I felt like playing any of Kimwa's silly games.

But I guess my experience had frightened Kimwa as well. She stopped daring me—at least for a time.

Chapter Six

The Storm

By the time I was able to move about again, Mother
was busy fishing. We had been spending our time
down by the stream, not even bothering to return to the
den by night. I enjoyed the nights out under the sky, no
den to hamper our movement, no covering overhead
to shut out the light of the stars or the orange glow of
the moon.

The sounds of the night were different, too. I loved
to listen to the rustle of the dry leaves underfoot as
some little creature scampered along the forest floor
searching for food. I loved the sighing of the wind in
the tall fir trees. I loved the call of the coyotes from the
nearby hills—though their cry make Kimwa shiver.

But Mother didn't seem to miss the confinement of
the den. If she did, she did not discuss it with us. I
guessed that it was my fall that first kept her from
returning to the den to rest. Then it just seemed to be
accepted that it was quite safe to sleep in the forest.

We stayed close to the stream, Mother insisting that
I go back in for a soak now and then to keep the
swelling from my bruised body. As I felt better, I began
to walk with a little less stiffness and venture a little
further from the bed Mother had made me.

Mother often joined me in the stream. I think she loved the water. She would roll and play in it almost like Kimwa and I did. Then she'd shove her nose deep into the coolness until I was sure that she'd run out of air.

Of course she never did.

One day as I lay on the riverbank, soaking in sun after my dip in the cold water, I noticed Mother poised in the middle of the stream. She was quiet and motionless. Only her eyes darted back and forth and I could tell that she was intent on something. I knew better than to call out to ask her what she was doing.

But Kimwa didn't.

"What're you looking for?" she shouted above the ripple of the stream.

Mother just lifted her head and glared at Kimwa and I guess that she knew she had spoken thoughtlessly. She moved off a few paces and lay down on the soft grass, content to lick her scuffed paws in silence.

Mother shifted her position to another spot in the stream and started her silent vigil again.

I watched. It was a lazy way to spend an afternoon, but I still didn't feel like doing much anyway.

Even though I had been carefully watching Mother I almost missed the sudden swing of her large paw. I did see something shiny lift from the water and land with a thump on the shore beside me. Mother was close behind it, placing a large paw on it before it had a chance to move.

It tried to move though. I saw a tail lift up, then whack back down and Mother silenced it with a quick swat.

Mother lifted her eyes to us then and we knew that it was okay to move or speak again.

Kimwa came forward quickly and beat me to Moth-

er's side. I was still moving slowly.

"What is it?" asked my sister.

Mother beamed. "A fish," she stated.

"What is it for?" asked Kimwa.

"For dinner," said Mother.

I was there by then. I looked down at the big, shiny thing under Mother's paw. It was strange looking. Nothing like the bugs or grubs that we had been enjoying in the past. Nothing like the tender plants, either.

"Try it," urged Mother.

I moved closer. It wiggled. I moved back. I wasn't taking chances with the strange thing. If it should decide to attack, I would be defenseless. I couldn't move as quickly as Kimwa or Mother.

But Kimwa didn't seem worried. She moved right in and reached a nose to the wriggling fish.

I don't think she cared much for the smell, for she pulled back slightly and waited for Mother.

Mother didn't keep us waiting long. She flopped down on the sand of the shore and began to dine on the fish. Kimwa watched carefully for a few moments and then reached out and took a lick. Mother pushed the fish within her reach and Kimwa licked her lips and took a tiny bite.

"It's good, she said, and mimicked Mother by flopping down on her little tummy on the sand and reaching out for another bite of fish.

I decided that it was my turn and moved in to push Kimwa to the side. But Mother would not allow my bullying—even if I had been hurt.

"You come to this side," she told me. "There is plenty of room for all of us."

I went around and carefully lowered my body to the sand in stretched-out fashion. I pushed my nose forward and sniffed. Then I stuck out my tongue and licked. Soon I was feeding on the fish along with Mother and Kimwa.

It seemed that Mother was still hungry after the fish had been devoured for she went back to the stream again.

Kimwa and I both lay quietly, giving our paws an occasional lick as we waited in anticipation for a bit more dinner.

It seemed to take Mother forever to get that next fish, but when it landed with a thump on the shore, it was Kimwa who reached it first.

But Kimwa wasn't as skillful as Mother in pinning it down—though I must give her credit for trying.

She ran to where the fish was flopping and bouncing on the sand and reached out a small paw to hold it, but the fish was stronger than Kimwa and caught her off-guard. With a flick of the large tail it lifted Kimwa right off the ground and deposited her again in an upside-down position. I couldn't help but laugh—and laughing hurt my sore ribs.

Kimwa got up and gave me a scowl. She had been good to me since I had been hurt—but I could tell by the look she sent me that the favors were about to stop. She frowned at me and picked herself up from the sand while Mother pinned the fish to the ground and prepared for another feast.

Kimwa and I didn't even have to be invited. We joined Mother immediately, enjoying the fresh taste of the trout.

From then on, Mother fished daily. Fish became an important and enjoyable part of our diet.

In a few days we saw a sight like nothing I had ever seen before. As we went to the stream to drink and wash and get our breakfast, the stream was teeming with the shining pink of fishes.

"Mother, look!" squealed Kimwa. "Look at all of them. We'll never be hungry. Never!"

"They are salmon," explained Mother. "They will only be with us for a few days and then they will be gone again. Only a few will remain behind, here and there, along with other, smaller fish."

"Where do they go?"

Mother shook her head.

"Somewhere," she said.

"Do they come back?" I asked, fearful that we would never enjoy salmon again.

"Oh, yes. They come back. But in fewer numbers. The fishing will never be this good again until next year at this time."

"Then we'd better hurry," sang out Kimwa and plunged into the water.

It was funny to watch Kimwa. She was determined to catch her own fish, even if they were as big as she was. Time after time her paw flashed through the air and time after time she missed.

On one occasion she did manage to snag a fish, but it was so big that she was unable to hold it.

Mother smiled at Kimwa's attempts and threw a fish out on the shore for each of us, one right after the other. Swish. Swish. Swish.

We ate salmon until our sides ached. It was delicious and I hated to think that they would soon be gone.

But Mother was right, as always. Just as the hundreds had suddenly appeared, so the hundreds were suddenly gone and we were back to long, silent fishing again.

Mother spent hours in the stream fishing. She also spent hours showing us how it was done. I was feeling almost as good as new now and I joined Kimwa in the creek, patiently staring into the clear water, waiting for a fish to draw near enough for a strike. It was long, tedious work and on more than one occasion, Kimwa and I both gave up, climbed to the shore and basked in the sun, leaving Mother to do the fishing.

Still, I was determined that I would be the first one of us to catch a fish. I didn't say anything to Kimwa, nor did Kimwa say as much to me, but I could see the dare in her eyes even though she had not spoken it.

When Kimwa napped, I would sneak back into the stream again and take up my post. I was determined to land a fish while she wiled away her time sleeping in the sun.

But day after day I was a failure. Mother kept encouraging me.

"Be patient," she'd say. "Fishing takes skill—and practice. Lots of practice."

So I practiced. I sat motionless in the water or leaned on a flat rock and watched the swirling stream and the circling fishes until I was dizzy. Then I swatted and swiped and lunged and grabbed, but all to no avail. I was discouraged and frustrated.

"I bet Kimwa will be first again," I complained to myself.

We had both been fishing with Mother, and Kimwa had come so close to actually landing the fish she had hooked that I felt my whole body tremble. I was sure that she'd land the next one.

Just then a small fish circled close to my paw. I was afraid that it was going to dart off again. Then it circled once more and came in closer. I was sure that it was just curious and I couldn't help but wonder how many times its mother had told it to stay away from strange objects.

But the fish seemed intent on finding out what it was that was dangling in the water. It moved closer—but it was not on the right side of my paw.

I waited breathlessly. It was hard not to try to move my paw around behind it—but I had tried that many times and it had never worked. The fish always darted off, just as mother had said they would.

So I sat quite still, holding my breath and making myself be patient.

And then the fish slipped around my paw and came at it from the other side. It was just what I had been waiting for. With a quick flash of the paw I lifted the fish right out of the water and onto the shore.

"I got one! I got one!" I was yelling excitedly and I didn't even think to run to shore to make sure that the fish didn't flop its way back into the water again.

But Mother did. Before I even moved, she was on the shore, one big paw almost covering my tiny fish.

Kimwa's eyes snapped and I knew that she was disappointed that I had beaten her.

"It's so tiny you'll eat it in one gulp," she challenged.

"It's still a fish," I threw back at her.

Kimwa followed me out of the stream to where Mother held my fish. Mother seemed very pleased with my effort.

"Good job," she said to me, her eyes shining. "I saw you wait. I think you will make a fisherbear."

I grinned, then looked at Kimwa with pride in my eyes.

"See," I wanted to say to her.

"Here," said Mother. "Why don't you enjoy this one all by yourself?"

I flopped down on the sand and stretched out. I wasn't really hungry. Mother had already fed us well, but I made a great show of enjoying my little fish, all the time casting glances toward Kimwa to be sure that she was watching me.

Kimwa lay on the sand and groomed herself for several minutes as I nibbled and smacked over my dinner. When she arose to go back to the water she moved close enough to whisper savagely, "Bet I'll catch the biggest one," and then she was gone.

But our fishing for the day soon ended. A large thundercloud had been gathering overhead and a loud crack of thunder sent Mother splashing from the water with Kimwa close at her heels.

We had experienced many rains before. They came often, swelling the streams and washing the dust from the hillsides. Kimwa and I enjoyed the rain. We played in the rivulets and teased the animals that ran for cover. But this storm was unlike anything that I had ever seen before.

I had never heard such crashing and rumbling of thunder. Even the trees about us seemed to tremble, and then the wind increased until the trees were more than trembling. They were swaying back and forth, struggling to maintain their upright positions. A few were torn from their moorings and came crashing through the timbers as they fell noisily to the ground, wrenching other trees and shrubbery as they fell. And all the time the wind whipped against us, the rain slashed down upon us, drenching us to the skin in no time and tearing at our fur and faces.

It was a frightening thing. Mother drew us further into the forest seeking some kind of shelter from the angry storm. But the swaying, creaking trees overhead brought no sense of safety. On and on Mother plodded, but it seemed there was nowhere to go to get away from the storm's fury.

I could tell by the tension in Mother that she was worried, but she did not speak to us about it. Instead, she began to move carefully through the dense undergrowth, urging us to follow quickly.

We tried to keep up but it was hard going. The wind tore at us even in the shelter of the forest trees and the ground underfoot was already soft and slippery.

I heard Kimwa whimper above the din of the storm. I forgot about her last challenge. Now I was concerned that she would be able to keep up with Mother and me. I dropped back beside her and gave her a nudge of encouragement with my nose.

"I'm scared," she murmured.

"Mother will take care of us," I tried to assure her and Kimwa nodded and kept on running.

We were soon out of breath. Mother had been plunging through the forest, not even stopping to sniff or to listen. Now she pushed up another small hill, panting hard in spite of her size and strength.

"We're almost there," she turned to say to us and we pushed on.

Then Mother was poking and pushing at a tangle of branches in front of her and there we were, right back at our den.

"Get in. Quickly," she told us, and Kimwa and I both rushed through the opening at once, almost getting struck in the process. Then Mother pushed her way in, clearing more of the opening as she did so.

We were safe—and we were in a dry place. Mother began to move things about, making more room for us to lie down together. She didn't even bother to close the door behind us. Overhead the storm still raged. I could hear the thunder and the beating rain. Flashes of lightning danced all about us. Now and then a tree was torn loose and with a screech, came crashing to the ground where it lay trembling and moaning in the tearing rain.

"What will we do?" I asked Mother.

"We'll wait here until it stops," she answered simply and the calmness of her voice reassured me.

"Is it gonna stop?" whimpered Kimwa.

"It always stops," said Mother, "sometime."

We snuggled together and Mother dried us off. Then she held us close and nursed us while the storm still beat at the door of our den.

"Try to sleep," Mother encouraged, but I was sure that I'd never sleep as long as the storm thundered above us.

But I guess I must have become used to the noise and commotion for when I lifted my head the sun was shining again. I could hear the birds singing and the squirrels chattering. But even as I looked out the open door I could see that our world had changed again. Though it was no longer storming, the trees still dripped with steady droplets and here and there big trees were down, often taking with them smaller trees and bushes that had surrounded them.

"What will happen to the trees?" I heard Kimwa asking Mother.

"They will become logs," answered Mother. "It will take a long time, but the day will come when they will be homes for ants and bugs and beetles. Then they will be a food source for many of the creatures who live in the forest. The forest wastes nothing."

I was relieved to learn that some good would come from the storm.

"Now come," said Mother. "We slept through the night and it is time to find some breakfast."

"Where are we going?" wondered Kimwa.

"Back to the stream," said Mother. "We have two fisherbears in the family now. It should be easy to get breakfast from now on."

I knew that Mother was paying me a nice compliment and I couldn't help but give Kimwa my smug look.

"I'll catch the biggest one," she whispered in my ear and then we were off, following Mother.

Chapter Seven

Danger

We fished all morning. Kimwa and I fed on the fish that Mother caught and then went back to our own fishing. I knew that Kimwa was determined to out-do me and that made me too impatient to be good at fishing. But then, maybe Kimwa's impatience matched my own, for she lost fish after fish. It was almost noon before I finally snagged one. It was a good deal bigger than the one that I had caught the day before and I was quite proud of myself. I even remembered to dash ashore and hold the fish from flopping its way back into the stream.

I saw the determined look in Kimwa's eye and the stubborn set of her chin and knew that she was out to make good her challenge. I watched it all out of the corner of my eye as I feasted on my latest catch.

I had just finished my meal and was busy licking up when I saw Kimwa slightly shift her position. Her eyes were gleaming and I followed them to a shallow pool beside the rocks where she was outstretched. To my horror, a large glistening trout was circling slowly, studying Kimwa's dangling paw. I knew that the fish was much larger than the one I had caught.

For a moment I froze. My thoughts were racing round and round in my brain. Kimwa had beat me in racing. She had beat me in log rolling. I couldn't let her beat me in fishing, too.

I jumped from where I had been resting and splashed my way toward her.

"Seen anything yet?" I called innocently.

It worked. The big fish darted off to deeper and safer water.

Kimwa's head came up. I could see the anger in her eyes.

"You did that on purpose," she yelled at me. Then instead of calling for Mother as she had done in the past, Kimwa flung herself at me, her teeth bared and her short hackles rising.

I was caught off-guard by her sudden attack and before I knew it I was thrashing about in the stream, Kimwa on top of me, snarling angrily.

"Stop," I screamed. "Stop! You'll drown me."

"Don't care," shouted Kimwa. "You scared my fish on purpose. You knew I could beat you. You knew." And she continued to nip at my ears and cuff me on the side of the head.

I'd had enough. With one quick movement I flipped out of Kimwa's grasp and then it was Kimwa who was in the stream—and then it was me. We rolled over and over, splashing and thrashing and sending spray flying in all directions.

Then I heard Kimwa giggle. Our war had suddenly turned into a game again. It seemd that it was always that way. Neither of us could stay angry for long.

For several minutes we continued to wrestle and roll in the cool stream and then Mother called and we had to quit.

"Well, you did scare my fish on purpose," Kimwa insisted again as we dashed for shore and ran to catch up to Mother.

I grinned sheepishly. "I know," I admitted, "I'm sorry."

Kimwa took the opportunity to bite my ear one last time, but it was a playful nip and didn't really hurt at all.

By the time we caught up to Mother she had rolled a log and we were much too busy to continue the conversation.

It started to rain again. Not like it had the day before with thrashing winds and whipping rain—but steadily, from a dark and sodden sky. Mother looked up every now and then as though to study the situation. I was wondering if she was thinking of returning to the warm den and I really didn't want to. I didn't mind the rain on my coat.

All day it rained and all day we continued to forage for food. Darkness came early and we found a spot protected by large fir trees and bedded down. When we awoke it was still raining. We all were hungry so we headed for the river again.

Kimwa did catch her big fish. It was not quite as large as the one she had nearly taken the day before, but it was a good bit bigger than either of the ones I had caught. She looked at me with a gleam in her eyes and I nodded, conceding defeat.

Again we spent the day trekking through a watery world. Rain continued to fall at a steady rate and we splashed up little sprays of water with every step we took. The branches overhead were little protection as they dripped almost as steadily as did the clouds in the sky. We tried not to bump against the bushes, for they sprayed us with water if we did.

Mother grumbled a lot that day. I knew that she didn't care for the steady rain. I knew that she was hungry, and feeding in the rain was much more difficult. I knew that she worried for our safety as well, for it was much harder to hear and to smell when in the midst of a rainstorm.

Still, we plodded on, grabbing a bite here and a bite there. Every now and then Mother would stop and roughly shake her heavy coat. Water would fly in every direction and Kimwa and I would scamper away so that we wouldn't get even wetter than we already were.

At last Mother grunted her disapproval of the continued rain and changed direction. I knew that she was again heading for our den but by now it seemed like a good idea, even to me. Kimwa and I followed close behind her, anxious to get in out of the wet and the cold.

It was hard traveling. The fierce winds had brought down a number of large trees and whenever one fell it always took several others with it. They were a tangle of branches on the forest floor and we had to continually re-route around them and then find our bearings again.

It wasn't hard for Mother. She seemed to know where she was going at all times—but it would have been terribly confusing for me.

At last we reached our den. Mother led the way. But when she stuck her nose into the small enclosure I heard her grunt of displeasure.

"What is it?" Kimwa whispered in my ear. "Has someone stolen our home?" By now Kimwa was shivering with the cold.

I wasn't close enough to know why Mother was so unhappy, so I stepped forward a few paces and stuck my nose in the den. It was then that I saw what the problem was. No other animal had stolen our property. I was quite sure that they wouldn't even want it as it was now, for the floor of the once-snug home was covered with water.

Mother grunted again.

"We'll have to climb higher," she said to us and nuzzled me with her nose, then turned to Kimwa.

"I'll warm you up just as soon as we find a suitable place to rest," she promised and Kimwa tried to stop her little body from shaking so that Mother wouldn't worry.

Mother led us uphill. It was the hardest climbing that Kimwa and I had ever done. If the weather had been nice, I would have enjoyed the adventure. We were seeing territory that I had never seen before. But you really couldn't get a very good look at it. It was raining much too hard and the darkness was closing in upon us, as well.

It seemed that we climbed forever. The trees were more scarce now with just a clump here and a clump there. More and more rocks were about us. The jagged edges were hard on our feet. Still Mother led us upward and finally, when Kimwa and I were about to give up, Mother stopped at the entrance to a dark hole in the face of the mountainside.

"What is it?" asked Kimwa in a trembling voice.

"A cave," answered Mother. "I used to live here."

"Do you—do you think it is still empty?" I asked, knowing that other animals often took over vacated dwellings.

"Wait here," said Mother, "while I check."

She moved slowly forward then, sniffing and listening and looking for signs of another inhabitant.

After some time she turned to us. "It's okay," she told us. "Someone else has lived here since I did, but

they are gone now. Come in."

Both Kimwa and I bounded forward, happy to get out of the rain.

It took Mother a few minutes to scratch a bed together for us and then we all curled up together and Mother began to lick us dry and warm our bodies as we hungrily fed. I was glad that Mother had known about the cave. It had been a long, hard climb but we were dry now. I was sure that the rain would never bother us way up here. I snuggled up close against Mother and fell asleep. Kimwa finished her nursing and buried her nose in my fur.

"It feels good to be warm again," I heard her mutter and I wasn't sure if she was talking to me or to herself.

"Um-m-m," I mumbled back, too sleepy to even open my mouth, and I snuggled closer to Kimwa.

The next morning it was still raining. I knew that Mother was very hungry but, after one look at the falling rain and the dark sky, she turned back to our bed again.

"We'll just spend the day here," she said and curled up with us again.

It wasn't too bad for Kimwa and me. We were able to nurse whenever we wanted but Mother must have been terribly hungry. She didn't complain though and I guess she did manage to sleep a good deal.

When we awoke the next morning there was no sunshine streaming in our open door and I feared that it was still raining, but when Mother checked, she announced that we would be able to leave the cave.

When I joined Mother at the door I saw that the rain had stopped though the sky was still overcast.

"Is it going to rain some more?" asked Kimwa.

"I don't think so," replied Mother. "At least I hope not."

I hoped not, too. I was ready for a dinner of fresh fish or a few ants or grubs.

"Now follow closely," Mother told us as we left the cave. "The paths can be dangerous after so much rain."

"Where are we going?" asked Kimwa.

"Back to the stream—but it is a long walk so try to be patient."

Mother began to lead us carefully down the steep mountainside. I could see now why it had been so difficult climbing up. It was even steeper than I had realized the night before.

As we picked our way carefully down the mountain the heavy clouds rolled on and the sun came out to greet the world again. I was so glad to see it. The whole world looked different when the sun was shining.

We spotted a few other woodland creatures. Birds flitted here and there, startled by our sudden appearance. We were scolded by squirrels who felt that the whole mountainside belonged solely to them. Mother ignored their warnings but Kimwa shouted back that we had as much right to be where we were as they did.

We were traveling slowly, carefully, over the rocks and windswept ground, when I noticed a log lying off to my right. I was terribly hungry for something sweet and figured that I could flip this log on my own. I knew that it would only take me a few minutes to turn it over, quickly gulp down the contents underneath, and then dash after Mother. I decided to take those few minutes.

It took a bit more effort than I had imagined to roll the log over on its back, but when I at last had it turned there was even better hunting than I had expected. Bugs, beetles, and ants scurried in every direction and I was beside myself knowing which ones to catch first. The grubs could wait for later. They hurried nowhere.

It was delicious and I was feeling quite proud of

myself when I finished the last morsel. Still licking my chops, I raised myself to my hind feet to see just how far ahead were Mother and Kimwa. They had traveled further than I had expected and I knew that it was going to take me some time to catch up to them.

And then I noticed that Mother was angling back across the face of the mountainside again and I looked toward the spot where she seemed to be heading.

"If I take a short-cut, directly to that spot, I should get there almost at the same time that she does," I reasoned and I began a full-speed lope straight toward the spot that I had picked as our meeting point.

I had not gone far when I realized that the ground under my feet was not very solid. What had been rock, where Mother walked, was mud where I was traveling.

I was going at a fast lope and knew that I would be wise to slow down and take things more carefully. I braked—but my feet went right on sliding. Before I knew it I had slammed sideways into a rock perched on the side of the hill. It must have been sitting there precariously for it seemed to teeter as my weight hit it, and then it dislodged and began to roll down the steep incline, with me and my muddy paws sliding right along with it.

As we went, we gathered other rocks—and much more muddy hillside. Soon there was a whole cavalcade sliding down the mountain. We went faster and faster as we slid and I remember hoping that Mother and Kimwa were not somewhere on the trail beneath us. I was afraid that the slide would sweep them right along with it.

I was being tossed and somersaulted head over heels and front over back. I bumped and jostled and thumped along. My body, that had just been fully healed after the fall from the tree, was being bruised and banged all over again and there wasn't a thing that I could do about it.

On and on we thundered, rolling and pitching and slamming into one another as I slid.

At last there was a slowing down, a few final thumps and thuds and I realized that I had stopped.

I wasn't sure which way was up. I wasn't sure if I could move. I didn't even know if I was free or had been buried alive. I was half afraid to open my eyes for fear of what I might find.

I tried to move one paw. It wiggled slightly. I tried another paw. It, too, moved just a bit. The third paw. It was stuck fast. I tried the fourth. It hurt far too much to move.

I knew that I was in trouble. Big trouble. I didn't know whether to try to pull myself from the rubble around me or stay where I was. I was afraid that movement might start the slide again.

I lay there whimpering, wishing with all of my heart that I had obeyed Mother. But it seemed a little late to think about that now.

I did finally open my eyes. I didn't see sky. Nor did I see forest. I lay facing a pile of mud and rock that had me half buried. One of the rocks had my left hind paw pinned to the ground. It was that paw that held me tight. But it was my left front paw that was sending pain coursing through my body.

My right front paw seemed to be free. I lifted it to try to push some of the mud and forest debris away from my face.

I moved carefully, cautiously, I didn't want to start things rolling again.

At last I had cleared a bit of the tangle away from me. It was then that I realized that my back was wedged tightly up against the trunk of a large pine tree.

Other trees in the area had reached out to lodge a rock or a bush or heaps of the mud. I was sure now that it was the grove of trees that had stopped the slide from traveling further. I was thankful for the trees. I also noticed that the ground had risen upward slightly so that we had lost a good part of our momentum by the time we had reached the trees.

I felt a bit more secure now. I didn't think that the slide would start again, even if I did move about.

I reached with my uninjured front paw and began to push against the rock that held me prisoner. It would not budge. It didn't seem to have damaged my hind paw much and I noticed that I had been pinned along with the branch of a tree. The branch had taken most of the weight—but I was still stuck fast.

I decided to work on the rest of me. I wriggled around until I could move my free hind leg hoping to get my feet under me so that I would be able to brace myself for further effort. That leg moved just fine, but the effort of movement sent such a shiver of pain through my front paw that I could hardly stand it. I knew then that I must lie still.

Then an awful thought went spinning through my mind. "If I do lie still, I will surely die right here where I am, pinned by the big rock beside me. Yet if I try to move it is going to hurt—something awful."

I really didn't have very good choices.

Chapter Eight

Mother

I decided that I had to move—regardless of the pain that it would cause me. There was no way that I wanted to lie there on the mountainside and die all alone.

I began to struggle to free myself. The pain was so great that I could only work for a moment at a time and then I would have to rest and try to find enough strength for another try.

I managed to wriggle and work my way until I was flat on my back staring up at a bright sun that flooded the wet world with welcomed warmth. But the sun was too bright for my eyes, and there was really no advantage in being on my back, so I began to work again to see if I could get myself turned over.

Besides, I had seen a large red-tailed buzzard hawk circling overhead—and I knew that buzzard hawks were carrion eaters. He wasn't a welcome sight for one in my dilemma. I didn't want to lie and watch him circle closer and closer.

I finally managed to half turn over. I lay there spent and scared, wondering how in the world I would ever get myself out of my predicament.

The day dragged on. The sun was moving from its position directly overhead and was slowly making its way toward the west. I kept straining to hear the sound of the red-tailed hawk's wings. Once I fancied that I heard them and I half-turned and screamed at the empty sky. The movement hurt me, and I screamed again in pain and anger.

I had been there for some time, when I sensed, more than heard, a movement somewhere near me. Something was coming my way.

I steeled myself, fearful that it might be the buzzard hawk. But it was a larger animal that made its way slowly across the sea of mud and rock. I could hear the sniffing now. I shivered. Perhaps a pack of wolves was moving in.

The sniffing drew closer. I tried to pull myself into as small a package as I could. I hoped that the rock would hide me and I wished with all of my heart that I had not cleared the mud and tangled rocks and branches from around me.

Then the light breeze brought a scent to my nostrils. I jerked at my captive rock, trying hard to hoist myself. The movement sent a stab of pain through my front leg.

"Mother!" I screamed. "Mother!"

I heard her answer with excited grunts.

"Over here," I shouted. "Over here by the rock."

And then Mother was there. Her nose pushed up against me, as she anxiously inquired as to how badly I was hurt.

"I'm pinned," I replied. I was in tears now. It was the first that I had cried. Even the pain had not had me whimpering.

"This rock," I sobbed. "It's pinning my back paw and—and my front leg is—is hurt."

Kimwa was there then, poking her slender nose toward me, taking a consoling lick at my mud-covered face.

"We've been looking and looking for you," she told me.

At their arrival I had found myself wondering what had taken them so long, but at Kimwa's words I swallowed my incriminations and tried to blink away my tears.

It didn't take Mother long to move the heavy rock. Once my back paw was free I flexed it a few times and was relieved to discover that it was still in working condition even though it was a bit stiff and sore.

But my front leg was another matter. When Mother gently helped me over on my stomach and urged me to try to stand, we found that the leg had been broken.

"You'll have to hop," Mother informed me. "You must get to safety."

I did hop—but, my, it hurt.

Mother led the way to the stream, though she didn't head for our usual spot. She chose instead a place closer to our present location so that I wouldn't need to travel as far. She tried to pick an easy path for me and she stopped often to let me rest. My damaged front paw dangled in front of me and with each hop that I took, the pain shot up my leg.

It took us a long time to reach the stream. As we picked our way slowly through the forest I was fully aware of several other painful parts of my body. It was hard to push myself onward. Mother would give me a few moments to rest and then she would urge me on again.

I was so thankful to see the stream ahead, though it was different than I had expected it to be. The water rushed and tumbled and spilled over the banks, sounding angry and hurried in its downward plunge. It was not the clear shining water that I was used to, but was dark with the stains of mud. I turned to Mother, questions in my eyes.

"It's from the heavy rains," she told me. "In a short time it will be back to normal again. But we can still use it. Try that sheltered pool just beyond the rock."

I hurried toward the small pool Mother had pointed out, my leg and body throbbing with each hop. I lowered my tired, bruised and muddy body into the stream and let the cool water ease the pain from me.

I lay there for a long time before I even tried to move. At last I crawled slowly up on the bank and stretched out with a groan on the grassy slope.

Mother had fished nearby. She saved me a portion of the fish that she caught and brought it to me, asking me how I felt.

"Some better," I answered, but I knew that Mother could still detect the moan in my voice.

I did manage to eat. The fish tasted so good. I ate hungrily and then I remembered that it was my greedy appetite that had gotten me into all the trouble in the first place. My appetite and my disobedience. If I had listened to Mother and followed her carefully down the mountainside like I had been told, I would never have crossed the dangerous ground that Mother had purposely avoided, and ended up with a broken paw and a bruised body.

I knew that Mother was likely thinking the same thoughts as she moved over beside me and began to gently lick the wounds that caused me such pain.

"We'll have to move again soon," she said softly. "You can't spend the day here."

I nodded. I knew that she was right. This was a strange part of the stream and it might be someone else's fishing hole. They would not take kindly to us using it without their permission.

Kimwa came to nuzzle me. "Poor Natook," she crooned. "Poor Natook."

I appreciated Kimwa's sympathy, but I didn't want her sentimental comments to cause Mother to remind us both that it was my own fault that I was in the state I was in.

"I'm ready now," I said, lifting myself slowly to my three feet and I began to move forward so that Mother would know I was willing to travel on.

She took the lead then, calling for us to follow closely and Kimwa and I fell in behind her.

It was slow traveling. By the time we had reached the spot where Mother wished to bed us down, the stars were blinking in the sky and the moon was directly overhead, smiling down upon the forest trails.

Mother selected a place in a dense thicket not too far from our usual fishing hole and we snuggled up together and were soon asleep.

Kimwa had a habit of pressing close in her sleep and more than once I was awakened by the sharp pang in my paw as Kimwa unknowingly bumped me. I would cry out in pain and pull away and Kimwa would waken, mumble a sleepy "sorry" and move back from me. I knew that she didn't do it intentionally—but it hurt just as much as if she had.

When we awoke Mother led us to our own spot at the river. My leg had become more swollen while we slept and I was anxious to get it back in the cold water.

I couldn't fish, so I didn't even try. Mother provided fresh fish for me and I ate hungrily after I had soaked for some time in the stream. Then Mother felt that we should move on and do some foraging deeper in the forest. She knew that I would be hampered in my running, should it be necessary for us to do so, and climbing a tree would be impossible for a time.

As we traveled, Mother turned over logs for us and ripped aside bark on dead trees so that we could get at the food supplies. Under one tall pine she found a delightful anthill and with a few swipes of her giant paw, she laid bare the inside of the dwelling, causing hundreds of confused ants to scurry aimlessly about. We had a delightful lunch there before moving on.

Kimwa and I were no longer the small skinny cubs that we had been when we had first moved out of our den with our gaunt mother in the spring. We were much larger now and our bodies had taken on a fuller look, covered by a glossy, smooth coat. Mother looked much better, too. Her sides were sleek and rounded and her coat had lost its rumpled look. Mother had provided well for all of us over the months of spring and into summer.

"If it wasn't for my paw," I grumbled as I followed jerkily after Mother, "we would really be in good shape."

But I remembered whose fault the accident had been and I didn't complain as I hustled along to try to keep pace.

Kimwa was good to me. She let me have the choice morsels under the rocks and logs. She didn't even tease or challenge me to games that she could have easily won.

I was thankful for her kindness and resolved that if the tables should ever turn, I would be more considerate of my little sister.

Just as we were about to enter a small meadow, Mother stopped short. Her head jerked up and I saw the danger signal flash to Kimwa and me. We both stopped mid-stride, perfectly still and perfectly silent.

Mother rolled her head back and forth, sniffing and listening, then she rose high on her hind legs and peered through the growth into the meadow before us.

With a satisfied grunt she fell back onto all four and called us forward.

"It's just a couple of deer," she said, matter-of-factly, and began her way into the meadow.

I hadn't seen deer before to my knowledge and I felt an excitement fill me in spite of my aching limb.

They were much bigger than squirrels and they didn't bounce from tree to tree. In fact, they walked on all fours just like we did.

As we entered the clearing, they lifted their heads and stirred nervously. I could see them sniffing the air and tossing their heads. One decided not to wait around to see if we meant them harm, but bounded off toward the cover of the forest.

The other stood her ground, her nose lifted high, her large ears flicking this way, then that. She shifted her weight on long, slender legs, but she did not run.

I wanted to just stand and stare at her. She was so different from anything that I had seen before, but Mother was moving on, completely oblivious to the stirring of the graceful animal, and I knew that I must follow her. At our slow progress, the deer began to move slowly forward also, its head held high, its nostrils flaring.

I felt more awkward than ever as I hobbled along behind Mother, one paw dangling and the rest of my body bouncing along with each step. The deer seemed to glide across the clearing as it slowly made way before us.

"It's beautiful," whispered Kimwa beside me and I realized that I wasn't the only one impressed by the animal before us.

It was soon gone from our view but Mother didn't seem to notice. She had found another promising log and had stopped to struggle with it in an effort to shift it from its position. It was larger than the logs she usually tackled and I wondered for a time if she was actually going to be able to unsettle it.

She was, but it took her longer than it usually took her to turn a log. When she did get it flipped, there wasn't much there to eat. I guess maybe everything that lived under the log had already been warned by the commotion and had hidden in the small holes in the ground.

Mother grunted her disapproval at the scanty fare and moved off to find something better.

Kimwa and I followed. Kimwa trying her hand at peeling dead-tree bark or turning small logs or rocks as we wandered.

Mother decided that it was time for one last trip to the stream before we took cover for a nap. She said that I needed to soak my leg again. I didn't argue. It was hurting pretty bad. It had been a long day and we had covered a lot of territory.

But when Mother led us to the stream I was surprised at how close by it was. It seems that we had circled, never getting too far away from where Mother knew I would need to be at the end of day.

I bathed and soaked again, feeling the cool water lift some of the pain and swelling from the damaged leg. Mother allowed me ample time and then suggested that we be on our way.

She found a different spot for our bed. I guess she didn't want any of the forest creatures to know just where we were, nap by nap. We curled up together again, me with my broken limb held away from the squirming Kimwa, and slept until the sun had swung to the west and was about to disappear for another day.

Chapter Nine

Misadventure

The weeks passed quickly. Day by day my leg
improved. Mother still insisted that I have my morning
and evening soaks in the cool stream. I never argued. It
always seemed to ease the discomfort. Then gradually
the leg was not hurting me as much. I even forgot at
times and put my weight on it. I quickly lifted it
again—and winced just a bit, if Kimwa was watching. I
didn't want to forego her good-natured pampering.

I was more and more captivated by the other animals of the forest. We saw the deer again on more than
one occasion. I always wished that I could have a chat
with them, but Mother seemed to frown on such a
venture and gently steered Kimwa and me in another
direction, or ignored the deer and let them go on their
way.

"Why don't we ever stop and talk to them?" I asked
one day.

Mother seemed not to hear my question.

"Why don't we?" I insisted.

She looked directly at me then, her eyes small in her
large head.

"Why?" she asked bluntly.

I was taken aback by her gruff response.

"Well—well—why not?" I stammered.

"Because they are not our kind. We have nothing to say that is of interest to them—nor they to us."

It seemed silly to me that animals would live in the same forest and not speak to one another. I had noticed the squirrels and the deer chattering on occasion.

"The squirrels talk to them," I informed Mother.

"The squirrels chatter with everyone who comes their way," Mother answered not sounding too impressed with the squirrels.

Kimwa looked at me with a slight shrug of her slim shoulders. I could tell that she shared my feelings but she didn't speak up. I let the matter drop and we both ambled off together to tip over a small rock nearby.

As we fed on the exposed lunch, Kimwa shared in a whisper, "Why don't we just talk to the deer when Mother isn't looking?"

I gave Kimwa a dark look. I had learned that it was not wise to disobey Mother. My leg was a grim reminder, even though it was healing nicely now.

"I forgot," muttered Kimwa, "we would be disobeying, wouldn't we?"

I thought about that for a moment and then shook my head slowly. "I don't know—for sure," I answered. "Has Mother ever really told us that we couldn't talk to strangers?"

"We-ll," drawled Kimwa, "not really, I guess."

"Then I guess we wouldn't really be disobeying her."

Kimwa's eyes twinkled and I knew that she could hardly wait for an opportunity to present itself.

But the days passed by and we did not see the deer family again.

I was really disappointed. I had so wanted to have a short chat. At least to say, "Hi. How're you doing? Do you like it in the forest?" but the deer seemed to have vanished among the tangle of trees.

Kimwa and I did take every opportunity to chat with the squirrels, though. They seemed to know all of the gossip of the woods and were more than glad to share it.

"Where are the deer?" I asked them one day.

"Oh, they have gone up higher where the grasses are growing now," the big red-tailed squirrel answered me. "They only feed down here until the food is plentiful higher up."

"Why?" I asked him.

He flicked his tail. "How should I know?" he barked at me. "That's just the way it is, that's all."

"What about the rabbits?" I asked next.

"They're here. You just don't see them as much, that's all. Food is all around them and they stay close to their nests."

I had been aware that there were still rabbits about us. I had heard them thumping in the night on a few occasions, but it had been several days since I had actually seen one.

"Do you ever move?" I asked the large squirrel.

"Move?" he shouted at me. "Why move? This is my forest. No reason to move. I was here first. If anyone is to move, it's you bears. You came in here after I was already here. If things—."

I backed away and decided I should check to see where Mother was. She was feeding not far from me and I determined to go see if she needed me. The squirrel was still scolding and calling me names as I moved off.

"No wonder Mother doesn't bother with them," I

said to myself as I traveled out of earshot.

Mother invited me to share her anthill as I came close and I moved in to enjoy the feast. Kimwa was off a short distance feeding on some succulent plants that grew by a bog.

"Did you learn anything?" Mother asked candidly.

"No," I admitted, blushing a bit that she had noticed my conversing with the squirrels.

"Nor will you," she said simply, and let it go at that.

I moved over to join Kimwa. She let me push my way in and steal some of her grasses.

I had made up my mind that I wouldn't spend my time with the squirrels in the future—at least not that particular squirrel. "Surely," I thought, "they aren't all so pig-headed and bigoted. But if I get a chance I will chat with other members of the forest."

But there didn't seem to be many creatures around us. Oh, there were always signs that animals had been there, but by the time Mother and the two of us arrived, it seemed that they had always disappeared. I began to think that perhaps the forest animals did not particularly wish to speak with us.

It angered me slightly. What possible reason could they have for snubbing us?

As I was ambling along after Mother, thinking my grim thoughts, a movement in the bushes at the side of the trail caught my eye. I stopped short and sniffed the air, turning my head first this way and then that. There was some forest creature close by. I felt excitement, and then I reminded myself that whoever it was would most surely high-tail it out of there before I even had a chance to introduce myself.

I lifted myself onto my hind legs so that I could get a better look. I at least wanted to see it dash off.

But it wasn't dashing anywhere. Oh, it was moving,

to be sure, but it was proceeding with a very slow gait.

I dropped back to all four and eagerly galloped into the bushes to get acquainted. Here was someone who didn't feel himself above speaking to a bear.

He didn't exactly run when he heard me approaching at a quick pace, but he did hasten his step.

"Wait," I called after him. "Wait! I want to talk to you."

But he didn't wait. He hurried even faster.

"Wait!" I called again. "Let's chat."

He was heading for a grove of trees nearby. I knew that if he reached them he would soon disappear from sight. I changed my direction in the hope of cutting him off.

He seemed nervous about what I had done and quickly swung about and really hustled on, his small funny body rocking back and forth with each hurried step.

"Wait," I puffed, out of breath. "Where're you going?"

I was almost to him when he seemed to disappear under a mound of bristly stubble.

"Hey," I cried in disappointment. "Where'd you go? I just want to talk. Come out from under there" and I reached out my nose to push the prickly mound off the little fellow.

Before I had even reached him, there was a quick movement and something hit me across the nose. It was a tail. A very prickly tail. I jerked back with a squeal, crying loudly for Mother.

I could hear the brush breaking as she sped to me and before I could even back away a few paces she was there at my side. The strange ball still lay curled up before us. I was sure that Mother would slap it all across the meadow for what it had done to me.

But as soon as Mother slid to a stop, she looked first at me and then at the little heap before us—and she backed up a pace. She grunted in anger, but she did not attack it.

"Come," she said to me. "Come." I followed her, both of us backing away from the presence of the round prickly ball.

When Mother felt that it was safe to do so, she turned and walked quickly away from the spot.

I was still whimpering. My nose was still stinging. As soon as I thought we were away from the danger I flung myself to the ground and reached up to rub at the spot.

"Don't!" cried mother. "You will only make it worse."

"But it hurts," I cried.

"Of course it hurts. You have quills in your nose."

"Quills? What are quills?"

"From the porcupine. They curl up into a ball and strike with their tails. They are full of quills that stick when they hit."

I began to cry harder, wondering how I would ever be free of the quills that were smarting my nose.

"Come here," said Mother and she sprawled on the ground. I threw myself down and crawled to her in obedience.

One by one, Mother drew the quills from me with her teeth. It felt like my nose was afire each time that she pulled another one. I was whimpering and crying with the pain but Mother continued until each quill had been removed.

"We need the stream again," she said with a sigh and I thought of the cold water and couldn't wait to thrust my burning nose into its depth.

Mother called Kimwa and we moved quickly toward

the stream. Mother didn't tell me to never, never tangle with a porcupine again. I guess she knew that I didn't need the warning. One experience with a porcupine was quite enough.

"What did he say?" Kimwa asked as she splashed beside me in the stream while I cooled my throbbing nose.

"Nothing," I mumbled.

"Nothing? You mean he wouldn't even talk?"

"No," I said in anger.

"Then what did you say?" she prompted.

I just stared sullenly at Kimwa.

"Nothing," I answered.

"You must have said something," she insisted.

"I just said, 'wait so we can talk,' " I told her.

Now it was Kimwa's turn to stare. "Then why did he get so angry?" she persisted.

"I don't know. I didn't do or say anything," I maintained.

"He wasn't angry," said a voice beside us. It was Mother. I hadn't realized that she had been listening.

"Then why—?" began Kimwa but Mother interrupted.

"He was frightened," she said simply.

"But why?" demanded Kimwa. "Natook wasn't going to hurt him."

"He didn't know that. And bears are much bigger than porcupines."

I hadn't thought of that. I hadn't meant to frighten the little fellow.

"Their quills are their only defense," Mother went on. "They can't run fast, they aren't big and strong enough to fight, and many of the forest animals like to dine on porcupine."

I heard Kimwa gasp. Neither of us had thought of that.

"Bears?" asked Kimwa candidly.

Mother just nodded. "Some bears—sometimes."

"But what about all the prickles?" I couldn't resist asking.

"Oh, they aren't prickly all through. Just the top part. Underneath they are quite nice. Almost like fresh fish."

Kimwa and I looked at each other.

"No wonder they don't want to talk," said Kimwa in a whisper.

I nodded.

"Well, I won't try talking to one again," I admitted. And then I hurried to add, "But I don't plan on trying to eat one, either."

Chapter Ten

Good Pickin'

It was several days until my nose had stopped its stinging. Mother and Kimwa took good care of me during that time. They were careful to push the food to me so that I wouldn't have to thrust my nose into places to draw it out. We made frequent trips to the water as well, so that I might soak out some of the poison from the quills. Soon the swelling in my nose went down and then it started the healing process.

Next it began to itch. I wasn't sure which had bothered me the most. The stinging or the itching. I rubbed it in the dirt and scratched it against tree trunks until I nearly wore the skin off, but still it continued to plague me.

I was so thankful when the effects of the quills had finally passed. I guess Mother was too. She let me go back to fending for myself again. With my leg now healed and my nose back to its rightful state, I was finally able to go back to fishing.

We all enjoyed our meals of fish, but I guess Mother wished for a bit of a change in her diet for she announced one day that it was time to move.

"Where are we going?" asked Kimwa.

"To the berry patch," answered Mother. "I can smell them in the wind."

Kimwa and I had never seen a berry patch, but if Mother smelled them and if Mother decided that they were worth traveling for, then we were quite happy to go along.

"I wonder what kind of creatures berry patches are?" Kimwa asked as we traveled side by side.

"I don't know," I answered truthfully. "I have never heard Mother speak of them before."

"What if they are like porcupines?" asked Kimwa with a glint in her eyes.

I gave her a cuff. I still wasn't ready to be teased about porcupines.

"You oughta get a few of those in your snout and see how you feel," I hissed at Kimwa.

Kimwa just laughed and ducked to avoid my second cuff. The first thing we knew we were rolling over and over in the grass again. Kimwa started to giggle and soon I was laughing too hard to be able to wage a serious fight.

"Come," we heard Mother call and we stopped our romping and began to run after her.

Mother stopped now and then to feast on the product of a log or stone that she just couldn't resist. We joined her without invitation. She accepted our pushing and shoving to get the biggest share of the findings and then she went on without comment when the snack was over.

We traveled down the hillside, across the stream at a place we had not visited before, up the other side and through the forest. At last Mother began to slow down and Kimwa and I both knew that she was taking careful stock of the area to be sure that it was safe for bears.

When we came to a small clearing Mother stopped to go through her routine. She lifted her head to sniff in each direction, then she listened carefully and lifted her huge body up on her hind legs to look all around us. Kimwa and I followed her movements. We were all satisfied that there was no danger when we proceeded cautiously into the clearing.

There were small bushes in the clearing and a new odor that I had never smelled before. It was sweet and tangy and it made my nose twitch. I could see Mother's nose twitching also.

"Where are they?" I asked Mother.

"Who?" she replied, sitting right down on her haunches and using both front paws to strip some bluish-purple things off nearby branches and direct them to her mouth.

"The berry patches," I replied.

Mother was much too busy enjoying her find to answer right away.

"Where are the berry patches?" I asked again.

"This is the berry patch," she said with her mouth full, swinging one large paw to make a full circle.

I looked about me. I still didn't understand. But I guess Kimwa must have. She had sat right down beside Mother and was busy pushing the plump juicy things into her mouth as well. Juice was dripping off her chin.

"Aren't you going to try some?" asked Mother.

I nodded dumbly.

"Here," said Mother, thrusting a paw full of the pickings toward me. "Try some berries."

It was then that I understood that we were there to eat the berries—not the berry patch.

The first bite had me hooked. I had never tasted

anything so delicious. No one even talked from then on. We were much too busy trying to get our fill of the delicious fruit.

All afternoon we continued to feast. As the day drew to a close I looked around me. I was afraid that we had nearly exhausted our supply. Mother must have read my thoughts for she said around a mouthful of berries, "There are more—in other places."

I nodded, pleased to hear it.

"There will be more here, too," went on Mother. "In a few days, more will ripen. We can visit here again."

I was glad. I wanted to feast and feast on the succulent berries.

"Don't the other animals like berries?" I asked Mother.

"Oh, yes. Many of them do. But I guess we are the biggest animals in the forest that feed on them."

Mother didn't say so, but I gathered that our size gave us a bit of advantage in claiming the patch as our own.

We bedded down quite close to the berry patch. There was still some picking left—though it wasn't nearly as good as what we had experienced on our first day in the patch.

In the days ahead we did still make our trips to the stream and we did still eat on fresh fish and grubs and insects. And we did still catch an occasional frog or other creeping thing—but for Kimwa and I there was nothing that quite measured up to the berries.

Mother must have shared our feelings for she was quite willing to travel for many miles over the hillsides to find another patch. When we found one we stayed until we had licked the last bush clean. Then we headed back to the stream again so that we could wash down the last morsel with cool, fresh, mountain water.

I didn't bother much with trying to talk with the other creatures of the forest. I had decided that perhaps Mother's code of live-and-let-live might be the best way to go, but I wasn't about to ignore them if they should strike up a conversation with me, either.

I don't know that you can really say that I had a conversation with the blue jays. It was more like a shouting match—and since there were four of them and only one of me, though Kimwa did get in on it, I guess you might be able to figure out who outshouted whom.

It started one morning when we entered a berry patch that we had not visited before. I could smell the berries from way down the trail and I could hardly wait to get there. Already my tongue was fairly dripping in anticipation. We moved in cautiously and then, when we were assured that it was safe, we dug right in to filling our hungry stomachs.

I was just shoving a large pawful into my mouth when there was a screech like nothing I had ever heard before. It startled me and I scattered the whole fistful of delicious berries on the ground. I could have cried, I was so upset.

Mother must have heard the screech too. She was not that far away from me, smacking and licking as she scooped large berries into her drooling mouth. She seemed totally unconcerned, so I guessed that whatever the noise, we were in no immediate danger.

The screech came again and this time I looked up to see if I could find the source.

"What do you think you're doing?" came an angry voice from directly over my head.

It was a jay—and was he mad! His feathers were ruffled, his eyes flashing and I thought that he was going to attack me right then and there.

"What are you doing?" he screamed again.

I looked directly at him and shrugged carelessly as I had seen my mother do in the past. "Eatin'," I answered civilly enough.

He screamed even louder.

"Eatin'? Eatin' our berries?"

"It was my understanding that they belong to whoever finds them," I answered with my mouth full.

"Exactly," screamed the jay. "And we found them."

By now another jay had joined the first.

"We found them. We found them," she started to scream at me.

I stood to my feet and pushed the last berries into my mouth. As soon as I could manage it, I yelled right back, "So did we. So did we."

"Well, we found them first," the first jay challenged, coming even closer on the branch of the tree.

I turned my back on both of them and kept right on eating berries. That made them even more angry.

"They're ours! They're ours! they both started to scream at once and then two more came to see what all of the commotion was.

"They're stealing our berries," they were told and that got the newcomers screeching, too.

I turned around to face them then and stood to my full height. "We are not," I shouted back. "They are just as much ours as yours—so there!"

My, what a fuss they made! They were so angry that one of them took a dive right at me, trying to clip my head with his sharp beak. I ducked. I didn't like the thought of having my head laid open by an angry blue jay.

I was about to duck and run when Kimwa joined me.

"Go away," she shouted on my behalf. "Go away

and leave Natook alone."

The jays did not seem the least intimidated by the pair of us.

"You go away," they shouted back. "This is our patch and these are our berries. Get out of here. Both of you."

"We won't," cried Kimwa and she reached up and took a swat at a diving bird.

That was too much for the jays. They all began to yell at the same time, screaming and squawking and making an awful racket. I just wanted to get on with the task of picking berries. We were wasting some valuable time.

But the jays weren't finished with us yet. They had their heads together and were chattering away and I was quite sure that they weren't planning a welcoming party. Soon the biggest one swung around to face us.

"This is your last chance," he hissed, "get out of our patch or—."

But he didn't say anymore. In fact a sudden silence hung over the clearing. I didn't understand it until I turned slightly and there stood Mother, still chewing her last mouthful of berries, her chin dripping juice but her eyes glaring. She lifted herself up on her hind legs and towered above the bushes, above the meadow, almost above the lone tree on which the jays perched.

The silence hung heavy for a few minutes and then the jays took flight. Mother said nothing, just dropped down on all four and resumed her feeding.

The jays waited until they were at a safe distance and then the noise started again. They were too far away for us to hear their angry words but they flung them back at us anyway.

"And you, too," shouted Kimwa after them.

I rolled over in the grass and began to laugh. I

laughed until my sides ached. Kimwa joined me and we rolled and laughed together.

I would have just kept right on laughing had not I been so anxious to feast on the berries. We soon stopped our giggling and began to stuff berries in our mouths again.

Mother paid no attention to our silliness. She was much too busy eating.

Chapter Eleven

Learning the Rules

I'm sure that we visited every berry patch in the vicinity over the next several days. We were scolded once or twice—mostly by jays or squirrels. A few larger animals complained somewhat but they moved aside when Mother entered the patch. The disputes over property rights never amounted to much.

I enjoyed the berries. Both Kimwa and I were growing daily. Our sides were beginning to bulge, rather than to dip in.

Still, I never could get my fill of the berries. But soon they were becoming fewer and fewer, and at length Mother gave up looking for the patches. What few scattered berries remained, we willed to the blue jays.

But I missed the berries. Oh, how I missed them. They had been such a delicious part of our menu for a few weeks and to give them up entirely was very difficult for Kimwa and me.

We resumed our hunts under logs, beneath dry bark and in the stream, but I couldn't put the sweetness of the berries from my mind.

And then Mother had another wonderful surprise for us.

We had been walking through the forest on our way to the stream when I saw Mother's head go up and her nostrils quiver. At first I feared that there might be danger nearby but she didn't seem at all alarmed.

She took a few more steps and then she stopped and lifted her nose again. This way and that way her head rolled as she sniffed first in one direction and then in another.

Presently she lifted herself up to her full height and sniffed and sniffed. I knew that she was checking for something but I had no way of knowing what it was.

I lifted myself onto my hind legs and began to sniff and search the wind as well. I could detect some new smell on the breeze but I had no idea what it meant to us.

Mother dropped again and began to move off toward our left and Kimwa and I quickly followed.

We hadn't gone far when she stopped to sniff again. Then she dropped back down, changed her course only slightly and was off again. I knew that she was on the trail of something.

She seemed very eager to get to where she was going and when she had taken a few more steps, she stopped and sniffed again. Then she studied a large tree that stood directly before us and soon began to slowly climb its trunk.

Kimwa and I had never seen Mother climb before. We were not surprised that she could do it—and very well—but she had not shown us this skill over the summer months. Now she climbed steadily upward, her lumbering big body lifting itself higher and higher into the tree. It seemed that she was making her way up toward a hole that showed in the dead trunk.

Kimwa and I gathered at the bottom, our eyes fastened on Mother, our mouths gaping open. We had no idea what would happen next.

But Mother knew exactly what she was doing. Straight for the hole she climbed and when she got there she reached in one long paw and scooped at the interior.

Her paw was empty when she pulled it back out.

Then Mother busied herself tearing away at the small hole with her jaws and her sharp claws. It was touchy work. Mother clung precariously to the tree trunk with three paws as she scratched and clawed away at the enlarging hole with the fourth.

She hadn't worked for long when Kimwa and I saw movement in the air around her. I couldn't figure out what the small, storming creatures were, but Kimwa whispered, "Bees."

"Bees?" I had been stung by a bee once when I was a very young cub and had sniffed at the flower where it was resting. It had hurt my nose and I had howled angrily. Mother had warned me about bees then and I had left them strictly alone ever since. I couldn't understand why Mother was breaking her own rule and stirring them up now.

Mother was shaking her large head. Bees buzzed all around her. I knew that some of them must be finding their target but Mother only grunted and kept right on digging at the hole.

Soon an opening large enough for her to reach deeply with her paw appeared and Mother braced herself, shut her eyes against the swarming bees and stretched to reach into the hole.

Her paw was not empty when it came out this time. In it she clutched something. Even from where we stood we could smell the sweetness.

Mother tossed what she held to the ground and reached back in again. Again she let fall what she withdrew. Again and again her paw dipped into the hole and again and again she dropped her find.

Kimwa and I still stood gazing upward, awaiting Mother's next order. But I was finding it more and more difficult to wait. The smell of whatever Mother had found was nearly driving me crazy. It smelled even sweeter than the berries that we could no longer find.

I guess Kimwa felt the same way, for she didn't even wait for Mother. I saw her clutch one of the prizes that Mother had tossed down and, flopping on the grass on her stomach, she began to lick at the contents with a long, eager tongue.

I couldn't stand it anymore. I grabbed up another of the pieces and stretched out beside Kimwa. It was better than anything I had ever tasted in my whole life.

I could hear Mother sliding down the tree, snapping off brittle twigs and small branches, but I didn't even look up. Soon Mother was there beside us, smacking her delight at the taste of the spoils.

We all ate until there was no more. Kimwa and I had a little row over the last small piece, but Kimwa won. She grabbed it quickly in her tiny teeth then ducked under Mother who had stood up to sniff the ground to be sure that we hadn't missed anything.

I didn't dare chase Kimwa once she had Mother's protection, so I growled angrily at her and plodded off a few feet to lie and sulk.

I was still licking my lips and my sticky paws, enjoying the last hint of taste when I looked up at Mother. Her left eye was swelling and she had several other lumps on her face as well. I knew that they were bee stings and that they must be smarting. Mine certainly had.

"Do you want to go to the stream?" I asked with concern and Mother licked the last morsel from her huge paws and nodded.

Kimwa followed close behind us. I figured that it was time to talk, now that the feasting was over.

"It was delicious, Mother," I praised her. "What was it?"

"Honey," she answered.

Her eye was really swollen now but she didn't seem to pay much attention to it.

"Honey," I repeated. "It sure was good."

Then I thought of something else.

"Did the bees want it too?" I asked Mother.

"I suppose they did," answered Mother and I saw the hint of a smile. I noticed another sting on the left side of her lip.

"Why?" I asked.

"They made it," said Mother simply.

"They made it? But how? How do they do that?"

I could hardly believe what I had just been told. Those pesky little stingers were actually good for something.

"They make it from the nectar that they get from the flowers," answered Mother.

"Could we?" I asked quickly, thinking how wonderful it would be to have an unlimited supply of honey.

Mother shook her head. "Only the bees know how to do it," she admitted.

I did so wish that the bees would share their secret. But at the same time, I didn't really expect them to be sharing it with us.

We reached the stream and Mother waded directly out into the cold water and plunged her head right into the depths. I knew how she felt. I had felt the same when the porcupine quills had stung my nose.

Mother stood with her head under water until I was sure that she must have drowned. Then she lifted it, snorted a couple times, shook some of the water from her and plunged her head under again.

We stayed in the stream for some time and then Mother headed through the forest toward a swampy area. We had been there with Mother on many occasions before but we had never seen her do what she did now.

She walked directly to a muddy bog and thrust her nose deeply into the mud, then she rolled her head back and forth, back and forth until her whole face was covered with the goo.

I was sure that she would want to head straight back to the stream so that she could wash herself, but she didn't. In fact, she told us that we would be retiring early and she set out to find a good place to bed down.

When we awoke, she spent some time in the water again and then she returned to the mud-bog and covered her face once more. She left the mud on for the rest of the day. By then it was dry and caked and we went to the river so that she could wash it off. She didn't bother to plaster herself with the mud that night. I noticed that much of the swelling had left her face. I guess she felt much better too.

We moved back down to the stream the next morning and Mother took a long bath, rolling and dipping and then lifting her head to cough and snort. After she was finished with the bathing she settled herself to fish. Kimwa and I both took positions for fishing, as well. Kimwa caught the first one but I was close behind. Mother didn't catch hers until we were almost done devouring our catch. I think that Kimwa and I both felt pretty good about that, though neither of us dared to say so.

We were about to leave the stream and go foraging when Kimwa lifted her head.

"Look," she cried to me. "Up there on the hill. Someone is coming."

I followed Kimwa's eyes and sure enough there was movement on the hill and it was coming toward the stream.

"It's another forest creature," went on Kimwa and she lifted her head to sniff for a scent.

I raised my head and sniffed, too, but the wind was blowing from the wrong direction.

"I suppose it will just run off like they always do the minute they see us," I said dejectedly. It still bothered me that I never got to talk to any of them.

We lay and watched the animal draw closer. Then it disappeared behind some small shrubs and was lost from view.

Still we stared at the spot where it had disappeared, hoping that it would keep coming our way. Mother was much too busy fishing to be aware of the approaching visitor.

We were about to give up, thinking that we'd never see it again when it suddenly appeared again. It was much closer now. Almost to the stream, and Kimwa cried out even as I jumped to my feet in excitement. "Look! It's another bear. Won't Mother be excited."

The bear was almost to us now, moving slowly, stealthily, sniffing the air as it approached.

"Wow!" I exclaimed, "Look at it. I'll bet it's even bigger than Mother."

Kimwa had risen to her feet, leaving behind the last of her fish dinner. She was backing up slowly, her eyes big, her mouth open.

But I was sure that we had nothing to fear. Here was one of our own kind. Here was another bear. I wanted to bound forward eagerly and welcome him to our forest—our stream—our fish dinner.

But before I could even move I felt something swish past me. It was Mother. She placed herself between the new bear and Kimwa and me and her hackles raised. She was dripping water as she hoisted herself to her full height and there was no welcome in her voice.

"This is our territory," she said coldly. "You are trespassing."

The other bear drew himself up on his hind legs, as well. He was taller than Mother. But Mother didn't seem to notice.

"This is my area," she said again. "Mine and my cubs."

The bear stepped back and eyed Mother coldly.

"Maybe I like it here," it said.

"Maybe I will change your mind," Mother warned, and Kimwa and I pulled back into a tangle of brush behind us, sensing the tension that suddenly filled the air.

"Maybe you will have to," the bigger bear challenged.

I knew then that something strange and terrible was about to happen, but I wasn't sure how it would all come about. Kimwa must have known it too for I felt her little body press tightly against me and she was trembling from head to foot.

Then with a mighty roar, Mother dropped back down to all fours and lunged at the trespasser. He was ready for her and we watched in horror as the two clashed, rolling and swatting as they warred for the rights of the area.

It was Mother who drew back first. I could see that her ear had a jagged tear but she backed off just enough to get her bearings and then she threw herself at the offending bear again.

Again and again they clashed, but in the end it was the stranger who turned tail and headed back up the hill, Mother sharp at his heels. Kimwa and I crouched together where we hid, wondering to ourselves if Mother would ever turn around and come back to us. Never had I seen her so angry.

But not many minutes had passed until we heard her coming. She was still scolding and threatening with grunts and snorts and Kimwa and I didn't know if we should go out to meet her or stay hidden where we were. Then she called us and we came trembling from where we hid. Mother was glad to see us and after nuzzling us with her nose and making sure that we were both safe, she headed for the stream again to cleanse and soothe her wounds.

It was some time later that Kimwa dared to ask the question that had been bothering both of us.

"Why couldn't he stay here, Mother? He was a bear like us."

Mother snorted. I could see the flash of anger again.

"This is our territory," she retorted. "He knew that. If I had not driven him away, he would have sent us off."

"But why?" I chimed in. "Why couldn't we all live here? There is plenty of water in the stream. There are lots of fish. There are—."

But Mother stopped me.

"There is never enough of everything for more than one bear in an area," she said flatly. "It is an unwritten law of the forest. Two bears do not share one territory."

"But we are three," cut in Kimwa.

Mother looked at us steadily. "For now," she said slowly, "you belong with me."

Her words sent a shiver through me. Up until that

time I had assumed that I would always be close to Mother. Her words seemed to say that it was not so.

"For now," she had said. What did she mean by that? I thought a good deal about it as I curled up tightly beside her later on. She had looked at Kimwa when she made her statement, but was she meaning me, too?

Chapter Twelve

Unwanted

The days were getting shorter and the nights cooler. Mother said that Fall had arrived. That meant very little to Kimwa and me but it seemed to mean a lot to Mother. She seemed almost in a frenzy to find food.

It wasn't that there was a short supply. The stream still held fish and the logs and rocks still produced insects and grubs. The berries were gone, but we had visited the honey tree on a couple of occasions—and then the bees seemed to pack up and move elsewhere.

But Mother rumbled through the forest like a locomotive, frantically rolling logs and digging up anthills.

One day I dared to ask her why she seemed so driven to eat, eat, eat.

"Hibernation," she answered with her mouth full.

"Pardon?"

"Hibernation. We need a good store of fat to get us through the long winter ahead."

I asked Kimwa later if she knew anything about hibernation but she just shook her head and stared blankly at me.

I noticed that Kimwa had a fairly good store of fat, too. I wanted to tease her about it and then I looked down at my own body. I really didn't have much room to talk.

Kimwa and I followed Mother through the forest on her hunting expeditions. She didn't keep as close an eye on us now and sometimes we were able to be on our own for several minutes before she'd lift her head and call just to be sure that we were nearby.

We took advantage of those times and did a bit of exploring on our own. Kimwa still dared me to do things—like walking the slender log that had fallen across the stream, and climbing a poplar sapling right to the tip and riding it on down to the ground. Our games were fun and we usually didn't suffer because of them. But now and then we went a bit too far.

Mother was very cautious about campers. I had the feeling that something had happened in the past to make her wary, but she never talked about it.

"Don't go near campsites," she had told us over and over.

"Why?" I wanted to know.

She just scowled at me as though she felt she didn't need any more reason than the fact that she told me so.

One day we were ambling through the woods, stopping here to grab some ants and there to feed on a few grubs when Kimwa stopped, lifted to her hind legs and began to sniff at the air.

I stopped, too, and stood upright. Mother was a good way ahead of us, tearing up an anthill.

Kimwa stood sniffing. Mother sometimes teased her about being the "nosy" one. She always seemed to smell things first. I think Mother was quite pleased with Kimwa's keen sense.

"What is it?" I asked, trying hard to smell something myself.

"I don't know—but it sure smells good."

And then a slight breeze rustled the leaves around us and I caught the smell, too.

It did smell delicious.

"Shall we check?" I asked Kimwa.

She looked ahead to find Mother. By now she was on her stomach, her tongue busily sweeping ants into her mouth. Kimwa gave me a nod.

We didn't need to go far. The odor led us just over the small hill to our right and down along the stream.

Mother had never brought us to this part of the stream before.

Before us were a number of strange creatures; different sizes, different shapes, some moving about, others motionless. But all most interesting. We stood watching, our eyes big with wonder.

"Campers," whispered Kimwa and I suddenly realized that she was right.

But the wonderful odor remained, tempting us, teasing us, inviting us to come nearer.

"We'd better go back," whispered Kimwa, shivering with excitement or fear.

I wondered where her boasting and daring had gone.

I gave Kimwa a sharp look and pulled myself up to full height.

"The smell is coming from over there," I whispered, pointing at a row of metal things that stood together close by. "We could run in, grab it and be gone before anyone notices."

Kimwa looked doubtful. I decided not to wait for her. I sneaked around in the bushes until I was very close to the spot and then dashed in, tipped one of the metal containers, shaking off its top and spilling its contents, grabbed a whole sackful of the tasty-smelling stuff and headed for the woods on the run. Kimwa was close behind me.

When we were sure that we were at a safe distance from the camp, I flopped down and with my paws and teeth, removed the outer wrapping from what I carried. Kimwa joined me. I shouldn't have shared. She had been so chicken, but I let her have some. Maybe it was just my way of boasting over what I had done.

It was delicious. There was many different tastes in what we consumed, all of them a bit different from anything we had tasted before. I couldn't help but think what a shame it was that Mother didn't take advantage of the camper's supplies. Especially with her getting ready for "hibernation" and all.

After we had licked the last of the food from our lips Kimwa and I hurried off to catch up to Mother. She hardly raised her head when we came puffing up to join her. We had seemingly gotten away with our little excursion.

But now that we knew about the campsite, we could not resist it. Our little raids on the garbage containers became more frequent and more daring. Every time Mother fed near the bend in the stream we looked for a chance to sneak off.

One day our bravery led us almost too far. When we reached the campsite, we discovered to our dismay that the metal containers had been moved. We had to circle around to the other side of the clearing and then sneak in closer to where the cans had been placed. Kimwa was nervous about going, so I had to go in alone.

"Hey," one of the campers yelled. "There's a bear."

"It's only a cub," someone else responded.

"Don't go near it," a third person warned. "Where there is a cub that size, there will be a mother."

I laughed. They didn't know that Mother was back rolling logs and lifting bark.

By then I had worked a lid off a can and was

removing a bundle of rich-smelling contents.

I hurried off to join Kimwa. "See," I told her. "I made it—and they even saw me. They didn't do anything."

I lay down to tear away at the package and Kimwa and I smacked our way through the whole thing.

"I don't know why Mother is so silly about campers," I said around mouthfuls. "There's all that good food—and they never hurt you."

"Maybe we should talk to her about it," reasoned Kimwa.

I didn't say so, but I wasn't sure that was a good idea.

After we had bedded down, Kimwa yawned noisily and then spoke in an off-handed manner. "Mother, I—I think that there might be some campers by the bend in the stream."

"Yes," said Mother. "There are."

"Do you think that we should go see what they—?"

"We should stay well away from them," said Mother firmly.

"But—," stammered Kimwa.

"No buts."

I had never heard Mother speak so forcibly. Then her voice softened, "Now go to sleep," she said and snuggled Kimwa up against her.

It was several days before Mother fed near enough to the campsite for Kimwa and I to sneak off for a quick visit. There was no movement about the place. I lifted my nose into the sharp autumn breeze and sniffed long and hard. Only a slight odor greeted me.

"Maybe they have all gone into hibernation," said Kimwa at my side.

"Well, the big cans are still there," I informed her. "That's all we need."

We were not as cautious as in the past as we entered

the campsite. It was filled with strange odors and we nosed our way around, sniffing at this and then at that.

We were able to climb over everything, checking the wooden tables, and hanging from the fireboxes. Then we realized that we were wasting precious time and hurried off to the row of large cans.

Much to our dismay the lids would not come off. We pried and pulled and yanked as hard as we could but nothing happened.

We were about to leave the site in disgust when I noticed a strange box-like contraption off to one side. As I neared it I could smell something. I decided to check it out. Perhaps we would at least get a snack—if not a whole meal.

Kimwa was still busy wrestling with the garbage can lids. She hated to be defeated by anything.

I felt a bit smug as I made my way to the box. I was the one who was the smarter, I decided. While Kimwa fought a losing battle, I was about to discover dinner.

The odor was coming from the far end of the box. I circled it slowly, hoping to find some way to reach the food without actually stepping inside, but the box was enclosed except for one end. At last I dismissed all caution and entered the box slowly, nose extended, tongue fairly drooling.

I found what I was looking for. In the rear of the box, dinner was waiting—but just as I reached out to lift it up, there was a loud clang behind me.

I jumped with the suddenness of it and wheeled around to run, but my nose rammed hard into a metal bar. I tried to duck under it but there wasn't any "under." The whole end of the box had been sealed off.

I whirled around the other way seeking a hole through which to escape, but as my nose traveled in a complete circle I found that all around me was the

same kind of tightly closed fence.

I started to cry then. I guess Kimwa heard me for I saw her darting for cover into the nearby bushes. I cried even harder, but Kimwa kept right on running.

Several minutes passed before I saw her peeking out from the shrubbery. Stealthily she came forward, her eyes dark with fear.

"Come here," I called loudly, fright making my voice tremble. "I'm locked in. Help me out."

Kimwa came to me then. Together we went over every inch of the box, she from the outside, me from within.

"Open it! Open it!" I kept urging her.

"I can't! I can't!" she whimpered. "I can't find any hole—or handle or—or anything."

I was really getting scared.

"There must be one," I insisted. "Look closer."

But Kimwa still could not find any way to open the box.

"Go get Mother," I said at last, feeling that Mother's wrath would be easier to accept then the confines of the box.

Kimwa ran then, and I paced back and forth, back and forth, waiting for the two of them to arrive.

It seemed forever before I smelled them coming. I didn't know whether to keep up my pacing or to crowd cowardly in a corner and sheepishly hang my head. I knew that it was my disobedience that had gotten me into trouble again.

I strained forward, listening and watching the bushes at the edge of the campsite. Then I heard Mother's heavy step and her angry grunts and Kimwa's whimpering cries of fear and just beyond the first clump of bushes I spotted Mother's dark body. But at that very same moment, there was a roar from the other direction and a strange animal, big and noisy came thundering into the campsite, sending clouds of powdery dust flying into the air. The strange animal had a mouth on each side that opened up and two campers stepped out.

"We got one," I heard the one camper yell excitedly.

"It's one of the cubs," the other nodded. "Too bad it wasn't the Mother. She must still be somewhere around."

I looked back to the woods. Mother was still there but she was backing slowly away from the campsite, her big head rolling back and forth from side to side.

"Well," said the first camper, "guess we'd better take care of this one."

"Hate to do that," said the first. "He's pretty small to be on his own."

"Well, we can't leave him here."

"Guess not."

And the next thing I knew I was being hoisted up in the air and then the box was shoved onto the back of the strange animal and soon we were hurtling off again, whipping up clouds of dust behind us.

I don't know how long we rumbled and rattled along mountain trails but at long last we stopped and the strange animal spit out the two campers again and they came around to lift me down.

"Sure wish we didn't have to do this," said the first one.

"Let's check and tag him," said the other one. "We'll just have to keep an eye out for him and if he seems to be in trouble we can round him up again and take him to the zoo."

I guess they decided to do that for when I awoke, after a dizzying sleep, I had a funny thing in my ear and a stinging in my left hip.

But the box was gone—and so was the strange creature and the two campers.

I was thirsty. Terribly thirsty. I stood to my feet, my head still spinning, wondering which way it was to the stream. The territory was new to me. None of the landmarks was familiar. I looked up at the sun that still hung in the sky.

"The stream must be this way," I reasoned and set off on wobbly legs.

As I traveled I began to gain strength. The strange stinging sensation in my leg soon stopped, but the thing in my ear would not come off no matter how I pulled and fought with it. I decided to leave it for Mother's sharp teeth and set out once again.

I don't know how far I traveled, or even if I was going in the right direction, but soon darkness settled in all around me and I was forced to rest. It was the first time that I had ever had to find my own bed and I wasn't too good at it. It was lonely sleeping all by myself, too. I cried as I curled up in a ball and tried to keep myself warm.

The next day I traveled again. I still had not found water and I was so thirsty that I could hardly stand it, but I kept on going, only stopping now and then to grab a few bites of food to keep me going.

I traveled all day and into the night but I wasn't sure that I was making any headway at all.

The moon was high in the sky when I finally sought out a bed. I was thirsty and tired and hungry—and very scared and lonely as I curled up that night. I wondered where Mother and Kimwa were. I wondered if they missed me or had gone back to feeding on grubs and trout. I wondered if I'd ever be able to find them again and the thought made me shiver and cry. Never in my entire life had I felt so miserable and alone.

Chapter Thirteen

Together Again

I did manage to find a drink the next day. It was not our stream. It was only a little trickle that made its way down the side of the mountain, but I was mighty glad to see it and spent many minutes quenching my deep thirst.

There was not even enough water to lie down and take a bath, but I poked my face into it as far as it would go and rolled it back and forth. Then I drank from it again, not knowing how long it would be until I found another drink.

I felt some better as I started off, but I was still scared and lonely.

"I must eat," I scolded myself, feeling the gauntness of my body. "Mother would scold me for not eating," and I set out to find food in one of the many places that Mother had taught me to look.

I did find things to eat. Ants, grubs, rose hips, edible grasses. It wasn't enough to fill the empty spot, but it did help to give me some strength. Then I started off again, running at an easy lope, making my way back down the mountain and to the east.

On and on I traveled, only stopping to drink when I found water and to eat when I found a food supply. I was getting thinner. I would not be in very good shape for hibernation.

But I was learning how to care for myself. I was forced to do a lot of growing up in those difficult days. I tried hard to remember every lesson that Mother had taught us.

I did not speak with the other animals that I encountered. In fact, whenever possible, I avoided them. I did not want to start any trouble that I wouldn't be able to finish on my own. Mother was not there to rescue me now.

Once, as I traveled by moonlight, I nearly crossed paths with another bear.

I had gone to a stream for a drink of water when when I heard the bushes snapping and breaking behind me. I stood perfectly motionless, staring into the semi-darkness, sniffing the air for a hint of who the new visitor might be. By the light of the moon overhead I saw a dark figure approaching the water upstream. I knew that it was another bear from the scent that reached me.

He was much bigger than I was. At first a thrill went all through me. Here was one of my kind—and then I remembered Mother and her savage fight with the trespasser and I realized that in this case, I was the one trespassing. It sent a shiver all through me.

I backed up, slowly, silently. If there should be a fight, I knew which of us would come out the winner—and it wouldn't be me. I had no intention of challenging the other bear.

I had almost made my escape when he spotted me.

"Hey! You!" he roared. "You're on my property."

I didn't even answer, just took off running as fast as

my legs could go. I heard him crashing through the bushes behind me. But I had a pretty good start and fright added speed to my heels. Besides, he must have known that I wouldn't be back and there was no need to wear himself out. The noise behind me quickly subsided and I heard a few satisfied grunts and then all was quiet.

I still didn't slow my pace until I had put more distance between us.

I was panting hard when I finally stopped running and so tired that I decided to find a safe spot and curl up for a nap. I didn't sleep for long and then I was up and on my way again.

I had been on my own for a whole week and I was getting thinner and jumpier all the time. I was beginning to think that I would never find Mother and Kimwa and my instincts told me that we had very little time left until Mother's time of hibernation.

The air held a chill and the brisk wind tugged and pulled the few remaining golden leaves from the baring tree branches and hurled them to the forest floor. They crunched and crackled underfoot as I walked and I would have enjoyed the sound had I not been thinking such troubling thoughts.

"I'm lost," I whined. "I can't find Mother and I can't find our territory and I'll never, never find home again. I'm lost!"

I whimpered softly as I trudged along, feeling terribly sorry for myself.

I had just rounded a clump of bushes when my nostrils picked up the slight odor of bear on the wind. My head swung up and my body tensed. I was just ready for flight again when I heard a loud squeal. "Mother! Mother, come here quickly. I smell Natook."

I couldn't believe my ears. I rose upright onto my

hind legs and peered off in the direction of the sound.

Then I heard a familiar grunt and Mother spoke to Kimwa. "Where? Where is he?"

"I don't know," answered Kimwa excitedly, "but just a moment ago the wind—. It came from that direction and I smelled him. Honest! I'm sure it was Natook."

I was off on the run then, directly toward the voices. As I bounded through the bushes that separated us, I found Mother, hoisted on her hind legs, stretching her nose in the air, sniffing eagerly in all directions.

She dropped down on all four when I came hurtling at them and I heard her glad cry, "Natook, Natook, it's you," and both she and Kimwa ran to meet me.

My, what a welcome I received. We tumbled and rolled and kissed one another and laughed and cried all by turn.

"We've looked and looked," declared Mother and I responded quickly, "And I've been trying to find you for days."

"Did they hurt you?" Mother asked anxiously.

"Just—just this silly thing in my ear," I showed her.

She looked at me sadly. "I once had one of those too," she confided. "It took me years and years to lose it."

It was the first I noticed the ragged tear in Mother's right ear. I felt that I understood her reluctance to go near the campsite then, but I did not ask Mother for particulars about her experience. Besides, we had too many things to talk about.

But Mother did not let us talk for long. "Come," she urged us, "now that we are finally together again we must get on with our preparations for hibernation."

I looked at Mother and Kimwa. They had lost almost as much weight as I had. I knew that we had some serious feeding to do if we were to be fat and filled-out again.

The next several days were spent in frantic searching for food. It was so good to be back with my family again that I didn't even fight with Kimwa over the choicest morsels. But then she wasn't in a fighting mood, either. She shared with me every treat that Mother found us.

"Weren't you scared?" she asked me and I had to truthfully admit that I had been.

"What did you eat?" she asked next.

"The things that Mother has shown us."

"Fish?"

"No," I replied. "I never stopped to fish—but then I didn't find a stream large enough to fish in."

"Where did you sleep?"

"Wherever I could find a spot."

Day after day the grilling went on. Kimwa never seemed to hear enough about my adventure. Now that it was over, it wasn't as frightening to me as it had seemed at the time. I could even talk about it without my voice getting all trembly.

"Mother says that we must never, never go near campers again," Kimwa said solemnly.

"Don't worry," I shivered. "I won't."

"Mother was scared half to death. We began to think that we would never find you—that they had carted you off some place and locked you up."

"Do they do that?" I asked, my eyes wide with horror.

"They did that with Mother once. She was locked up for two hibernations before she got away again. She told me," said Kimwa with a knowing air.

I shivered again. It had been bad enough to be locked up for a few hours.

"Come," Mother called us, and Kimwa and I moved to obey. Mother had not been letting us get out of her sight ever since I had returned.

We moved back down to the stream. A cold wind whipped down the hillside and played hide-and-seek in Mother's heavy coat. I felt it ripple all along my back and it made me tremble slightly.

The trees were bare now except for the firs. They still clung stubbornly to their needles. The grasses beneath our feet had turned crisp and brown and were no longer good to eat. Mother didn't even pause to sniff at them as we passed on down the path.

When we reached the stream I noticed that little shallows at its edge were tinged with shining stiffness. I poked at it with a paw and it slivered beneath my touch.

"That's ice," said Mother. "It is starting to form on the water now. Soon the whole stream will be under its cover."

I poked at the ice again, thinking how strange it was that the water should suddenly be turned to this funny solid stuff.

Later that day it began to snow. The large fluffy flakes came down from the sky, drifting around us like feather flowers. Mother sniffed the air a few times, then led us off to feed again.

We slept and ate by turn, spending only a few hours at each activity before switching again. Sometimes it snowed, other days the sun shone. Once the snow even disappeared entirely—but it wasn't gone for long. Soon it was back again, sifting in around the trees, gathering at the edge of the stream, piling up in drifts in the meadow.

I pondered a good deal about the mystery of the snow. The whole summer had passed by and I still hadn't discovered where it went when it sneaked away. Of course, there had been no snow to watch over the summer months—but I should have found its den or something, I reasoned.

But snow or no snow, we carried right on, eating and napping, napping and eating, until one day I sensed a new restlessness in Mother.

She sniffed the air, she lifted herself to her full height, she rolled her head and twitched her ears.

"We need to find a den," she said at last. "It is time."

"What about our old den?" I wondered aloud.

Mother seemed to consider that. The rain had spoiled our old den but surely it had dried out over the long, often dry, summer. Then she grunted again and spoke to me, "We need a larger den this year. You are much bigger now."

"What about the one in the cave up the mountain?" asked Kimwa.

"That's too far," stated Mother.

Kimwa and I decided to give up and let Mother do her own selecting.

"Come," she said to us and we obediently fell into step behind her.

Kimwa and I were soon to discover that Mother was difficult to please. She checked out several possible den sites before she finally grunted her approval and moved us in. Then she spent some time rearranging the interior and making sure that the exterior was hidden from view.

At last she settled down and fell asleep.

I wasn't ready for sleep yet—but I certainly had no intention of leaving the den. My curiosity had gotten me into too much trouble in the past. I wiggled some and Kimwa whispered in my ear, "Aren't you asleep yet?"

"Can't," I answered. "I'm not that tired."

"I can't either," said Kimwa. "Wanna play a game?"

I snorted. "You really wanna get us in trouble," I said to Kimwa angrily. "You know Mother would be angry if we left the den."

"I don't mean leave the den," said Kimwa defensively. "We can play a game right where we are."

"What kind of game?" I asked, thinking that it didn't offer much of a challenge considering Kimwa's games of the past.

"A 'can you remember' game," said Kimwa.

It sounded boring to me, but anything was better than just lying there.

"You go first," I prompted.

Kimwa thought for a minute and then asked, "Can you remember how Mother found the honey—and how many stings she got getting it from the tree?"

I remembered. I remembered Mother's swollen face and her trip to the stream. I remembered her mud poultices and how funny she looked with it smeared all over the sides of her face. I also remembered that Mother hadn't offered one word of complaint through the whole ordeal.

We giggled a bit and snuggled closer.

It was my turn.

"Can you remember," I began, "The big bear that tried to take our territory?"

I felt Kimwa shudder beside me. "I was so scared," she whispered. "He was bigger than Mother."

"But he wasn't as mad," I said, and we giggled again.

"Do you remember," said Kimwa, "the jays at the berry patch and how angry they were?"

We both laughed loudly now and Mother stirred in her sleep.

"Sh-h-h," I cautioned Kimwa and our game became

quieter again.

"Do you remember," I asked slowly, "the taste of salmon?"

Kimwa smacked her lips, paused, then asked with teasing in her voice, "Do you remember which one of us caught the biggest fish?"

I gave Kimwa a sharp jab in the ribs and she jumped. Then she poked me back and giggled again.

But I was suddenly feeling sleepy.

"Do you remember—?" I began, trying hard to think of another one, but I'm not sure if I ever asked the question or not. At any rate, it was a long time until I felt like waking up and when I did I was very, very hungry and Mother was poking me with her nose and saying that we needed to stir ourselves and get down to the stream. And then I realized that I was also very, very thirsty.

Chapter Fourteen

Another Spring

There was still a lot of snow on the ground as we left our den and headed for the stream. Mother plodded on ahead, breaking trail for Kimwa and me. We scurried along behind her, wanting to stop to sniff at things, but Mother was traveling much too fast.

I was surprised at how much Kimwa had grown over the winter but I guess that I had grown some, too. Mother didn't look quite as tall to me, but she was lean and gaunt again.

When we reached the stream there wasn't much evidence of water. It was still under ice and snow and Mother seemed quite displeased as she sniffed and pawed at it. Then she began to gulp down mouthfuls of snow and Kimwa and I tried some, too.

With an angry snort, Mother led the way back to the den, gulping snow again and again as she walked.

We snuggled up together and slept some more.

I don't know how much later it was that Mother stirred us again, and Kimwa and I arose sleepily to follow her. We noticed as soon as we stuck our nose out the door that things had been changing. Oh, there was still plenty of snow around but there was a different smell to the air, and birds and animals were stirring about in the trees.

We left for the stream at a trot and, sure enough, when we got there water was rippling along the edges.

Mother drank deeply before she turned to us. "There won't be any fishing yet," she said, "so we might as well move on."

Kimwa and I both responded eagerly. We were anxious to work the stiffness from our muscles and to see if the springtime held new things to eat or to explore.

We didn't find much that day to ease our hungry stomachs, but we ate what we could before returning to the den. The next day we foraged again. And the next and the next.

We spent several days alternating between the den, the stream, and the meadow. Each day seemed to be getting a bit brighter, a bit longer, and a bit warmer. Finally Mother announced that it should be time to fish.

The stream was open now, though there had been a snowfall just two days before. I don't know where the snow had gone, but it had disappeared again.

Now the stream rippled and gurgled with a new vigor, spilling over its banks in spots, then rushing on with increased energy.

Mother waded right out to the deepest point of our fishing hole and splashed and tumbled until she was quite satisfied. Then she took up her spot for fishing and Kimwa and I each found a suitable place as well.

It was Kimwa who caught the first fish. I thought she had just been lucky enough to be in the right place at the right time but I had to admit that she had learned well from Mother. Mother caught a large trout soon after and I chafed as I waited for my opportunity.

It wasn't long in coming and soon all three of us were busy munching on our dinner. It did taste good after the long winter of going without.

Our spring days passed by rather uneventfully. Kimwa wasn't quite as quick to throw out a dare. But then as the spring wore on, we didn't spend quite as much time in close company.

I was growing more and more independent. And Mother was granting more and more freedom to both of us, though I felt that Kimwa still clung to her more than I did. Perhaps my time alone the fall before had helped me to grow up.

Still, if we happened to get too far away, or spent too long a time on our own, Mother was quick to send out a call that had us scurrying back. It bothered me at times. I felt that I was quite able to care for myself.

I liked to roll my own logs and lift my own bark. I liked to dig my own anthill, and find my own plants. But all of the time that I cared for my own needs, I felt that Mother's sharp eye was always watching me.

So, one day in late spring, I purposely separated myself from Mother and Kimwa. I decided that the only way to keep from being closely "supervised" was to put some bushes between Mother and me.

I had to be quite sneaky about it, gradually, oh, so gradually, making my way a little further and a little further from where Mother and Kimwa fed.

At last I had done it. I was out of sight. I grinned to myself as I flipped a log. Never had the insects and grubs tasted so good. I continued on my way, nibbling at this and licking up that and all of the time I felt tremendously grown-up and self-sufficient.

I hadn't been gone long when I heard Mother call.

"Oh, bother!" I muttered, and lifted myself off the

ground where I had been reclining.

Then, with a shrug of my shoulders I flopped down again.

"I don't have to go," I told myself. "I'm big enough to care for myself."

So I didn't go. I just lay there, licking up ants and enjoying it until suddenly the bushes behind me parted and there was Mother, towering over me, her eyes dark with anger.

"I called," she said.

I cringed a bit.

"Didn't you hear me?"

"I—I—guess I did," I stammered.

"Then why didn't you come?" She was really cross now.

"I—I figured I could take care of myself," I said a bit too defiantly.

Mother gave me a firm cuff.

"As long as you are under my care you will do as told," she informed me and I nodded.

Suddenly I didn't feel quite so big or quite so independent. In spite of the fact that I had grown and was growing rapidly, Mother still towered over me.

"Yes, ma'am," I nodded, and stood to attention as I'd been taught.

Mother said no more but led the way back to where Kimwa waited. I didn't even look at my sister. I was sure that she would be grinning.

Later as we lay together resting after our foraging, Mother pulled me closer to her.

"Natook," she said softly, and there was understanding in her voice. "I know that this is a difficult time for you. It is true that you are growing up quickly. But it is also true that there are many dangers in the forest that you have not yet learned of. I hope that you will never have to face them—but if you should, I want you to know what you are to do."

I nodded glumly.

"The only way that I can be sure of that, is for me to teach you all I know—to show you what to do in dangerous situations," Mother said.

Another nod from me.

Mother waited a moment and then went on, "It is time for you to have more and more freedom—but not total freedom. Not yet. You are not prepared to be on your own—no matter how wise or adequate you may feel."

I lowered my head so that I didn't have to look into Mother's eyes.

"I'm asking you, Natook—to trust me. Please. Trust me. I will know when you are ready to be on your own—and I promise that I will not hold you for one day longer than I think necessary."

I didn't say anything, but secretly I wondered if I'd be an old, old bear by then.

"When you do leave Natook, you won't be coming back," Mother said solemnly and there was sadness in her voice. "You will find your own territory. You will be totally responsible for your own welfare."

My eyes must have widened. I had envisioned coming and going at will. Running off for an adventure here, then popping back to Mother, then taking a little journey there, and returning again to Mother. But it wasn't to be that way. When I left, I would be on my own.

When Mother explained how it would be, my impatience was quieted somewhat. I wasn't sure that I wanted to be totally alone. I had been alone before and I hadn't liked it one bit. Maybe I'd wait for just a bit.

I nodded in agreement. Mother seemed to see in my

eyes what she had been looking for. She reached out and licked me and snuggled me closer. For the moment it felt good to feel loved and protected.

The spring turned into summer. We fished and foraged and began to fill out. Kimwa and I were careful to stay well away from the campsite by the bend in the stream. Sometimes Mother ventured close enough for us to hear the calls of the campers drift through the greenery of the forest, but that was as close as we ever went and we did not stop or linger, but passed right by.

By the end of summer I was aware that Mother was indeed giving both Kimwa and me more time on our own, but always, after a period of foraging for ourselves, she would call, and we would respond.

Berry season came again. Mother took us to all the best patches and we filled our tummies on the delicious fruit. The jays still scolded. Kimwa and I took Mother's lead and completely ignored them. It made them terribly cross. I think that it was even more fun than when we had childishly shouted back.

Except for an occasional wrestle, Kimwa and I didn't share the same space much. We both had tremendous appetites and it seemed to take most of our time to satisfy them. We were very good at fishing. We caught our own almost every time that Mother took us to the stream. Mother seemed quite pleased with our accomplishments.

And then one day I took another important step into adulthood—or so it seemed to me. I sought out my own honey tree and raided it all by myself.

It was not an easy task. As soon as I neared the hole in the trunk the bees began to swarm. I kept right on crawling upward. They didn't think much of my visit and some of them got downright nasty. One got me on the side of the nose. Another nearly got my eye, then two of them landed on my ear and added to my misery. By the time I had extracted all of the honeycombs, I was an awful mess. But I didn't quit and I didn't fall. I kept clinging to the tree and raking the honeycombs from the nest.

At last I was convinced that I had it all and I withdrew carefully, lowering myself down the trunk of the tree.

It lay all around me when I reached the ground and I shut my right eye where the bee had stung me and pulled a large piece of comb to me. My, it tasted good. I was so proud of myself that I decided to call Mother and Kimwa to share in my find.

Mother came quickly. I guess she expected to find me in trouble again but when she smelled the honey and saw that I was safely on the ground she smiled proudly.

"Good work," she said and I felt my chest puff up.

"Have some," I said around my mouthful and Mother didn't wait to be asked a second time.

Kimwa came running up then, and she squealed with delight when she saw the treat.

Afterward Mother didn't even suggest the stream. She waited for me to make my own decision. After I had bathed my face in the deep, cold water, I was the one who led the others to the mud hole where I could apply the cool mud poultice to the stings.

They hurt—true enough—but I would have done it all again for another feast of that honey.

Not too many days passed by until my face felt fine again.

The summer turned into fall. I could smell it in the air without Mother even saying so and I knew that it was time to eat all we could, whenever we could, for as long as we could.

The berry patches petered out and we had to find other sources. It really wasn't too hard, as food was plentiful that year. I fed by myself mostly, though I knew that Mother and Kimwa weren't too far away. The deer sometimes drifted into the meadow while we were there, but they avoided us. Even if I was all alone, they skirted the area and it made me realize that I was getting pretty big. I no longer wondered why they didn't stop to talk. Deer were not too comfortable around bears. That was just the way of the forest.

But no matter how big I grew, the squirrels still chattered at me. From their position in the pine trees, they felt safe to say whatever they liked. It no longer bothered me. I just grinned at their threatenings and went on my way.

The leaves began to sift down from the tree branches and carpeted the forest floor with golds and reds and browns. I knew that it would soon be time for hibernating again. Mother didn't say anything about it, but I knew that she was thinking of it, too. I could tell by her hurried way of eating.

When we traveled to the stream together one day, I didn't wait for Mother to enter it first as I had always done. I waded out to the deepest part and splashed and tumbled about in the clear, cool water. Mother stood and watched me. Then I moved to a suitable spot and settled in to fish. It wasn't long until I had flipped one out on the bank with one quick swipe of my paw.

I lunged to pin it down so that it wouldn't return to the water and when it was still, instead of sprawling out to eat, I pushed it to Mother and went back to the stream to catch another.

Mother made no comment, just accepted the dinner, then tongue-washed her paws.

We walked back along the forest path toward the

place that Mother had selected for our nap. It was snowing gently by now and I lifted my nose to sniff into the wind.

In spite of the fact that I had grown up, I had still not discovered where the snow came from, nor how it sneaked away so silently. I coughed angrily, promising myself that someday I would learn its secret.

We reached our bed and Mother lay down and tucked herself in.

Kimwa snuggled up against her, but I remained standing.

"Mother," I said softly, "I think that I'll just forage for a bit longer."

Mother said nothing. Only nodded.

"I—I— may not be back tonight," I continued.

Mother nodded again, but I thought her eyes looked misty.

"I—I—," I didn't know quite how to say what I was thinking.

I guess Mother knew all about it, for she continued to look at me. "It's Time," she said with a nod of her head.

I swallowed hard. I wanted to go—I felt excitement coursing all through me. I didn't need to be fed and coddled anymore. I didn't need to share a winter den. I was a full-grown bear—well, almost. I could manage quite well on my own.

But I would miss Mother. She had always cared so well for me. She had always been there when I needed her—to rescue me or teach me or just to encourage and love me.

I would even miss Kimwa. She had been a good playmate. True, she had pushed a bit far at times, causing me to get into deep trouble. But we'd had fun together. I'd miss her.

I moved toward Mother and pressed my nose to her cheek.

"Be careful, Natook," she whispered.

"I will," I promised. "I will."

Kimwa seemed to sense that I was leaving. She rose to her feet. She was crying softly as she nuzzled up against me. "I knew you'd be the first to go," she whispered, then she sniffed back the tears and teasing filled her eyes. "I dare you to—."

I gave Kimwa a playful push before she could finish. "No more dares," I laughed, and she nipped me lightly.

I moved back to Mother and kissed her on the cheek again. I could taste the saltiness of tears.

"Be careful Natook," she whispered, "be careful," she repeated, as though she couldn't say the words often enough to impress them on my mind.

"I will," I promised solemnly. "I will."

And then I was ambling through the darkness alone. Mother would no longer be there to run to. I was an adult now and out on my own.

It was a frightening thought—but it was exciting too. I could hardly wait to find my own territory—to establish my own boundaries. The future lay before me and I was anxious to explore whatever it held.

Just before I passed out of earshot I heard Mother's voice one last time.

"Son—I'm proud of you," she called through the darkness. "Mighty proud."

I hesitated for just a moment and then I took a deep breath. I was ready to step out into the unknown, exciting world before me.